STRANGLED AT THE CINEMA
A HANNAH THE GHOST P.I. COZY MYSTERY BOOK 1

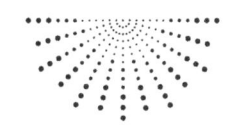

PENNY BROOKE

Copyright © 2021 by Penny Brooke

All rights reserved.

No part of this book may be reproduced in any form or by any electronic or mechanical means, including information storage and retrieval systems, without written permission from the author, except for the use of brief quotations in a book review.

This is a work of fiction. Names, places, characters, and incidents are either the product of the author's imagination or are used fictitiously, and any resemblance to any actual persons, living or dead, organizations, events or locales is entirely coincidental.

CHAPTER ONE

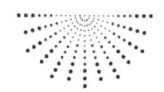

The buttery aroma of the popcorn gave me a little thrill as I stepped into the Yellow House on Main. This was my happy place: Colby Pointe's much-loved cinema and drafthouse, specializing in documentaries and independent films.

Then my heart sank, and I remembered: no more popcorn for this girl.

No more savoring the cool air in the Yellow House on a hot summer's night.

No more waves of anticipation as the music started and the beginning credits rolled.

Because five days ago, I died.

Now, I watched as Arnie Holmes set out the doughnuts on a tray and slid them into the case. He had only made two kinds, and not even the kind with sprinkles that always sold out first. He'd had strict instructions since I'd taken over at the snack bar: Always have the pink ones with the sprinkles. And with the chocolate doughnuts, put the icing on real thick.

I could see that he'd done neither. But I had to let that go. I had to let it *all* go, the good stuff and the bad.

The thing about it, though, was that I couldn't do it—which is why I hadn't passed to the other side like was supposed to happen. This no longer was my home, and yet here I was.

"Some of you drag your heels, which just prolongs the pain." Celeste flounced down onto a velvet couch beside the bar. She jiggled her leg impatiently so the sparkles on her shoe kind of danced in the light of the chandelier. I seemed to have drawn a rather cranky spirit to talk me through this *very* complicated and unexpected change. But it's not like you can fire your Orientation Specialist and Guide to the Beyond. Or at least I didn't think so; all of this was new to me.

This was not supposed to be what was on my mind this week. This was my week to work on publicity for Wine and History Thursday Nights. We'd have documentaries covering events from different decades, paired with exciting wines from our local vineyards. Today I was supposed to check the Q Boutique for something soft and silky and a little tight, something blue to match my eyes. Then tonight I was supposed to wear my dark hair down and wavy when I put on the dress to go out to the Greek place on the corner.

But I didn't get to do it. I didn't get to see how a dress like that would make Scott's eyes go all dreamy, which was my new favorite thing.

I was not supposed to be dealing with Celeste, who honestly made me think of that girl in fourth grade who always raised her hand and pointed at us when we chewed bubble gum or read a comic book instead of *Our Amazing Earth*. Now, she was staring absently at her long blue nails. I could tell she was aggravated I had somehow thrown the system out of whack. She was about my age—mid-twenties—with wild blonde curls around her face and a white and flowy dress.

But enough about Celeste! I was on a mission to soak in all the goodness while I still had the time. Which is why I ditched Celeste and slipped into Theater 2B.

Just as I was hoping, there was Scott: Second row from the back, a little right of center, where he always liked to sit. The loss of him filled me up as I drank in his broad shoulders and the familiar way he liked to tilt his head a little to the side.

Now, a certain type of woman would have been offended that her man was sitting *at the movies* five days after the vilest of creatures had strangled her to death in the parking lot outside. But I knew my man; I understood that Scott needed his familiar comforts more than he ever had. And the distractions on the screen, the temporary switch from reality to a made-up story, was how he'd always handled stress.

Scott Carlyle was the reason Celeste would have to drag me screaming from this place when I finally had to go. Scott was tall and well-built with soft black hair and green eyes a girl could easily get lost in. Best of all, he had a gentle spirit that could calm the impulsive, fiery parts of me. In short, the man was perfect. It was *finally* my turn for a lot of things, and romance was one. I had paid my dues. Name a category of atrocious men or nightmarish dates, and I could tell you a true story—starring me.

Then the gorgeous cop had kissed me, and we'd been together ever since, an all-too-short five weeks.

In fact, my life was finally on track in a lot of ways. One month before the kiss, I got a job at the movie house. A job at the movies! I watched films *for free* almost every day before or after work. Three weeks after that, I received a promotion to manager of special events and concessions. I could be creative with the foods, the festivals, the speakers. How perfect could it get?

The perfect job.

The perfect man.

Then as I was heading to my blue Camaro last week, there were two hands around my throat, and it was over, just like that. I had stopped in after work at Fallon Pharmacy across the parking lot. I had my little bag with nail polish and a soda as I headed to my car, texting Scott to say good night.

The thing about good luck is that it doesn't last.

How *dare* somebody take all of that away from me?

No matter what the rules said, I refused to leave until I knew who—and why. Scott would give it all he had. Scott was a brilliant cop. But he saw the best in people; he took people at their word much more than he should. He could mostly turn that off when he was at work, face to face with a guilty-looking suspect and some incriminating facts. But with our friends and neighbors, Scott was a trusting guy. And a little voice inside me said those hands around my throat were not a stranger's hands.

Whoever the creep was, he had come up from behind, and I couldn't see his face. I just remembered shock, a loss of air, then nothing.

Still, I had some thoughts on who. Not everyone in our sunny corner of central Florida had celebrated the good luck with which I'd been blessed of late. People could be petty—as if I had grabbed their share of the

"Happy Pie," and there was only so much of the stuff to go around.

Take Frances from next door, who had come after me, screaming mad, during what turned out to be one of my last days to be alive. Crazily, she seemed to think I *stole a check* out of her stupid mailbox in the middle of the day. What the heck was up with that? I was the perfect neighbor! Who took her paper to the porch when it was cold or rainy? Me! I picked her prescriptions up since she didn't drive at night. I had respect for my elders, just like I was taught.

But for some reason on that day, she came chasing after me like a witch on fire, a witch in fluffy house shoes and a shade of orange lipstick that could blind you like the sun. Her social security, she screeched, always came like clockwork the second Friday of the month. She had been watching from her window, and only two of us had walked past her mailbox on that Friday—the all-important *second* Friday of the month. First there was our postman—to put the check in, of course. Then I had come along with my pug, Cleopatra, to snatch that thing for myself, according to my neighbor.

I had seen signs before that her mind was slipping. Maybe soon, she would have figured out her check was only late or misplaced in her house. But that look in her eyes? Well, it still gave me a chill to even think about it. And I have to tell you, it takes a lot to chill a ghost.

Plus, there were those rumors about Frances's former life as a bill collector with rather terrifying ways of making people pay. But I believed her sons when they told me she had worked for thirty years at Abe's Fine Foods until the time of her retirement. That fit the Frances that I knew—well, most days at least. The Frances that I (mostly) knew was always cutting recipes and stories from the paper and slipping them into my mailbox. They always came with notes scrawled in her trademark pink ink with lots of exclamation marks.

Besides, she was so frail. It seemed hardly possible that I, a sturdy former soccer player, had been strangled by a ninety-something-pound octogenarian with two bad knees and one bad hip.

On the other hand, Frances Keene had two big sons, who had been locked up for fights and were protective of their mother. They were two giant mama's boys, who came to her house once a week for spaghetti night. Had they taken her at her word about the "stolen" check and come after me?

I wish there was a way to send a sign to Scott: "Look at Frances and her boys."

There had been a fire in Frances's eyes for sure, but the one who really let me have it—got up in my face and yelled—was that Bill Butterick from Doughnut Delights and More. His smallish eatery was across the parking lot from the movie house—and very, very close to where the "incident" occurred.

Okay, I was really sorry if people liked the doughnuts at the Yellow House more than they liked his. But my addition to our menu was absolutely not the reason there were no lines at his store. Instead of confronting me, perhaps he could have added some new flavors and not just had the two. Perhaps he could have stopped selling doughnuts that were stale? Or sold some other kinds of treats if he was going to advertise himself as Doughnut Delights *and More*?

All that I am saying is it was *not my fault* his business was down.

Of course, no one gets murdered over a thing like doughnuts or a single check that's late...do they?

Except Scott told me once that I would be surprised at how little it might take for some maniac out there to take a life. Scott worked a case one time where somebody was killed over the last pork chop on a serving platter. It was, in fact, that look into the pettiest and darkest parts of people's souls that drove Scott to the movies each week to forget.

That was our story started. Now it was up to Scott—and me—to figure out the reason our story had to end.

It could have been, of course, a stranger who had grabbed me, hoping I had cash or some jewelry to steal. But I had been feeling *vibes* from the people that I knew. Even on this day at the counter, Arnie had looked almost defiant as he skimped on the butter for the popcorn, as I had asked him not to do. He had made no secret he wanted the promotion that had gone to me.

I had felt the worst vibes from that blowhard cop Rick Trimble, who seemed to look at Scott as an obstacle to his chances to advance. I could tell that Rick felt threatened by my man, who he had known (and irritated) since the second grade. It probably didn't help that Scott had muscles and finely chiseled features while Rick was rather scrawny with a sprinkling of freckles and a constant look of confusion plastered on his face.

I could tell that Rick was majorly perturbed when I volunteered to oversee Kid Safe, a program in the schools that was a favorite of the chief of police. Scott, who liked the kids, would join in a lot to help. That, in turn, took the "spotlight" off of Rick, who liked to be perceived as the "exalted golden one." (Plot twist: he was not.)

But something more was up. Rick had really scared me with the way he always watched when I came by the station to drop something off for Scott. I had watched a lot of horror movies in the year before I died—we had held a Scare Fest in October—and I had gotten major "monster feels" from Rick. There was an anger in the man that seemed to go beyond who would be promoted when.

One night last week I was feeling shaky walking out to my Camaro after a late-night show. My heartbeat quickened even more when I saw movement near my car in the mostly empty lot. Trying to stay calm, I got my keys out for a quick escape and picked up my pace. But as I reached for the door, no one seemed to be around—until Rick's face popped up out of nowhere on the other side of the Camaro.

I stepped back and almost screamed, which made him chuckle in his kind of nerdy way.

"It's not the bogeyman. It's me. Gee, Hannah, get a grip." Once again, he laughed, but it was a fake mirth that didn't match the deadness in his eyes. "You really shouldn't walk by yourself this late. Bad things can happen, Hannah." The words themselves were innocent enough, but in his tone and in the way he stared a hole through me, I absolutely sensed a threat.

Three nights after that, someone at that same time of night, in that same parking lot, strangled me to death.

Bad things can happen, Hannah.

I hadn't had a chance to talk to Scott about that night with Rick, but he had concerns as well.

"Decent guy," he told me not that long ago. "He's just a little headstrong. Although, lately…ah, Hannah, I don't know." Scott had paused to frown.

"Go on." I had to prod. Scott liked to keep it "positive," not to criticize. Me, I was the opposite. I liked to keep it real.

"Lately, it's been weird," Scott said after a bit of hesitation. "Everywhere I go, he's there." He put his hands on his hips and sighed. "I see him in the gym when I go in to lift weights. I go out for a jog, and the guy is standing in the shadows, two houses down from mine. He's right there on my street."

"You see?" I touched his arm. "I told you he's a creeper!"

"Well, he had his reasons. Someone had reported a prowler on the street. There's been an uptick in those cases, so you be careful, Hannah. That's why Rick was there." But Scott had looked unsure. "Like I said, decent guy. But something's eating at him. There was a day last week I thought he was about to punch a hole right through his desk."

"Did you ask him what was up?"

"Something in his expression said to let it lie."

But to heck with that. I wouldn't let it lie. I vowed to keep my eye on Rick—and on the others too.

According to Celeste, the living couldn't see me.

Which meant I could see their secrets. I could see their true selves, the selves that only came out when they thought they were alone.

That was for later, though. For now, I would watch *Scott* just a little longer. I already missed him so much it literally hurt.

I slipped into the seat behind him. Except for the two of us, the theater was empty. The last showing on a Wednesday was never well attended, and this one had subtitles, which some customers complained was too much work. This one, though, was highly rated: a brother-sister journey across Tuscany and central Italy, filled with revelations about their family history and their hidden inner strengths.

I should've moved to sit beside him, I kind of wanted to, but I didn't dare. It would hurt too much when he stared quietly ahead—as if I wasn't there at all, which I kind of wasn't.

Then his shoulders heaved, and he quietly began to sob.

Instinctively, I moved beside him, longing for the comfort of having him close by.

Please don't let Celeste peek in and ruin this possibly last moment, I asked the universe. Celeste would have a fit. I was to stay away specifically from anyone and anything

I loved; it was these that kept me stuck here, in a place I couldn't stay, according to Celeste.

Well, it was easy, I supposed, for Celeste to talk. She had never had to walk away from a man like Scott! Defiantly, I slipped my hand in his and nestled my head on his shoulder. He couldn't feel it, but I could, and that would have to be enough.

Or he was not *supposed* to feel it.

"Whoa! What in the…" He jumped up in surprise. Then he stared at me, and his face went white. *"Hannah?"* A mix of shock, disbelief, and joy passed across his face like a jumpy movie reel. He blinked hard and then opened his eyes wide, as if he thought I might be gone when he opened them again. Next, he studied me as if he were staring at a puzzle—an illusion of some sort. "But Hannah, you are…" He closed his eyes again and shook his head, as if to chase away a dream. "I identified the body…I *know* that you are…" With wonder in his eyes, he reached out to touch my shoulder then my hair. "Hannah, are you real?" he asked in a whisper. "Or have I lost my mind?"

"I am here, and you can see me!" I ran my finger down his cheek, amazed. This was *not* supposed to happen. "Oh, I've missed you, Scott. Hello!"

Celeste had made it clear that the living couldn't see us. A very select few had an *inkling* of us watching over them or lingering to say goodbye, but we remained invisible, according to Celeste. Until now, she had been right. I had walked right past so many people I had known for years—or walked *through* them in some cases, which was interesting, to say the least. I could just watch and listen as they went about their business, gossiping about my murder, which was big news in a town where even burglary was rare.

Somehow, though, with Scott, there seemed to be a weak spot in the barriers between *us* and *them.*

Which was good. Which was amazing. I had more time with Scott!

I grabbed both his hands. "I can't stay for long," I told him urgently. "But let's go one more time to...well, to *all the places.*" Such a list of one-more-times was building in my head! I wanted to ride with Scott on his Jet Ski as the wind whipped back our hair. I wanted to sit with him on our bench and imagine lives for strangers passing by. It always was my goal to make him laugh at just one of my stories. Scott was serious and thoughtful, and just a small tug upward on his lips counted as a win.

This glitch, it was a good thing. There was time to say goodbye.

But Scott's look had turned to panic. This strong, muscled man—who could break up fights with one hand—looked like he might hurl or faint. "Not real, not real, not real," he whispered to himself before he got up and fled.

"Wait! Let me explain!" I ran behind him through the lobby. From the corner of my eye, I could see Celeste, her eyes opened wide and her mouth hanging open. Ignoring her, I turned toward Scott, who now had his hand on the door to the men's room. Now, normally, of course, I wouldn't follow him in *there*. Because, you know: *men's room*. But no one could see me except Scott! Being dead, I guessed, was not without its advantages (although I do not recommend it).

Then he seemed to change his mind and headed toward the door that led to the parking lot.

"*Do not* go after him!" Celeste grabbed my arm. "This interaction absolutely cannot happen, Hannah. I don't know how he sees you!" She ran her fingers through her curls and frowned. "There has been a major breakdown, it seems, in the system. Highly unusual."

Before I could respond, someone else was there.

Rick Trimble, of all people, showed up out of nowhere and grabbed Scott by the arm. "Feeling okay, buddy?" he asked him in a gentle voice. "Why don't you let me drive you home?" He led Scott to a bench.

Scott let out a sigh as he took a seat. "It's just impossible to think I will never see her, Rick. How can she be gone? I fell for Hannah hard. She was...*everything*." With his hands clasped between his knees, he stared hard at the floor. "Now my mind is just exploding. I'm hallucinating, man!"

"It's because you've had a shock," Rick told him in a soothing tone. "You need time to grieve. A massive, massive loss. Hey, let me drive you home. And then why don't you take a little time off work? I can cover for you. And maybe this week, I'll stop by. What do you say that you and me go out for a beer? Sometimes it helps to talk, to just let it out."

Scott nodded. "I appreciate it." And out the door they went.

Suddenly, it hit me: Was Scott in danger too from some rogue evil cop? I had to let him know what had happened in the parking lot with Rick just days before I died.

But, of course, he wouldn't listen. I would first have to convince this no-nonsense cop of mine that he believed in ghosts.

I followed them out the door and leaned sadly against the brick wall of the building as they made their way through the parking lot. Beside me, a big gingercolored cat was napping next to the ticket counter.

Nacho! My heart sank. I would miss Nacho too. We were just becoming friends. The stray cat was bashful when it came to interacting with the staff, but she wasn't shy about gobbling up the treats we brought her after hours from concessions. Her coloring made me think of our nachos, which we piled high with cheese. And so it was me who came up with the perfect name.

I looked back at her as I began my short walk home. "Goodbye, sweet girl," I whispered. "They'll take good care of you."

CHAPTER TWO

Frustrated, I decided to go home and eat a pint of caramel-toffee ice cream and flip through the TV channels. Although...there were lots of options now that I was kind of here and kind of not. I could slip into a room at the Azalea Inn, for example, with a massive bed, high-thread-count sheets, and champagne in the mini fridge, two crystal glasses on the counter. No three hundred dollars a night on your AmEx when you can't be seen—and there were always vacant rooms in the winter and the fall. Also, by the time any bill arrived from AmEx, I would be "no longer at address," "out of reach," and all of that.

On the other hand, I kind of longed for the old green couch at home with the cushions situated just the way I liked. My books were there, my comfy sweats, my t-shirts, so many things I'd miss that fit the shape of "me."

I liked being in my own home, where I had "woken up" on the day after I was killed. It started out as usual with the alarm, pre-set, blasting Katy Perry from my cell. Then I remembered details from a "dream" that seemed all too real in the morning light: hands pressing on my neck and the desperate need for air. A sense of horror lingered as I got up to make the coffee and get started on my day.

Something, though, was off. It intensified with the sound of weeping and voices coming from the den. When you live alone, that can kind of freak you out.

Then I recognized a breathy voice. Was that *Maria Claire*—here from Tallahassee—in my den?

Yes, it was my sister, pacing by the window and talking on her cell. "They *killed Hannah,* Janet; I cannot believe my sister's *dead!*"

I looked down at my wrists, at my hands, my legs. I ran my fingers down my arm. I still seemed to be myself. But a cold shiver pierced my insides as the awful understanding settled in. I don't know who was crying harder then—me or Maria Claire.

I was dead at twenty-six.

"I drove all night," my sister said, "to try to get to her in time, but two hours ago she died while I was at a rest stop. I had to have caffeine." She paused to blow her nose. "I wish I'd been a better sister!" Maria Claire wailed to her friend. "I did things I wasn't proud of, things she did not deserve. Like I went to the lake once with this guy she was seeing back in high school. When Hannah had the flu."

Maria Claire went out with Michael Grier? What the heck? But, of course, it didn't matter ten years later. We were grown-up women—and one of us was dead.

"Even as a kid, I made her play with Ken when we played Barbie wedding." Maria Claire's voice was growing more high-pitched.

Right away, I could figure out some things about this new status of "deceased." It was apparent, for example, that my sister couldn't see me. I mean, there I was—*right there*—while she went on and on about me being gone.

"Bad sister! I was bad," she said.

But, of course, she wasn't. Older by two years, Maria Claire had been my secret weapon, my first line of defense during any number of the cataclysmic dates I grew famous for. Years later we still laughed over Zeke Cooper, who had the nerve to whine when I ordered French fries, extra large, to go with my Coke.

"Who am I? Rockefeller?" he had asked with a honking laugh before he went on to flirt outrageously with a girl across the room.

My sister, working in the kitchen, heard all about it from our waitress. And the fries that Zeke ordered *for himself* were served up with the diner's special hot sauce—the scream-for-your-mama version—in his plastic ketchup cup.

After that, "Ketchup on the side," became our little code for a disaster of a date, even as we roomed together after college.

"Did you have a good time?" Maria Claire might ask when I came in from a date. "Or am I gonna have to pull out my special ketchup bottle?"

Now I grabbed some ketchup from the fridge and set it carefully beside her on the couch—to remind her that she had indeed been my protector, my best friend.

When she noticed it, leaned against a cushion two feet away from her, she did a double take. "That wasn't there before," she said to herself. "Where did that come from even?"

"Where did *what* come from?" asked the friend, whom my sister had on speaker.

"Janet." My sister caught her breath. "Do you think they can...send you signs? You know, from the other side?"

Janet's voice turned quiet. "I'd like to think they can."

"Hey, look, I have to go. I think...that someone's here."

"Don't let her friends and neighbors wear you out with visits," said Janet in a rush. "You need to get some sleep."

"Oh, no one's at the door. I just meant that...never mind. I'll talk to you soon."

Maria Claire checked into a hotel after that first night. She packed up my valuables and got my dog situated with Andi down the street, who always carried dog treats in her pocket. I'd snuck into Andi's every day to pet Cleopatra, who couldn't see me either but always wagged her tail when I was close. Dogs sense us better than most people can, according to Celeste. Their minds are not as muddled with unimportant stuff. For that and other reasons, dogs are thought to be "higher-order creatures" in the next world, where I am supposed to be, settling into my next life.

Now, as I arrived at home, Frances was adding blooms to the wreath of fresh greenery she'd hung on my door two days after my encounter with my killer. She seemed to have grown even frailer in the last few days. There were more gray locks escaping from her bun than still caught up in the messy twist. She wore a loose gray dress, a pair of tattered tennis shoes, and socks that didn't match—one blue and one beige.

Of course, I was swamped with guilt. In my head, I'd accused her of *my murder*, and here she was painstakingly tucking pink and yellow gerbera daisies into my wreath just so. I felt so bad I could die—which I guessed was an expression I should eliminate.

I'd told Frances once that the brightly colored daisies seemed like something that a fairy might choose for her crown. She had murmured something about thoughts "unsuitable" to a woman of my age. Then she had mumbled underneath her breath about the weeds in my own "sad patch" of withering impatiens. But I'd seen a tiny smile when she thought I wasn't looking. She took great pride in her gardens, which spread out behind and on both sides of her house. If someone tried to pick even a single bloom, they got the Frances glare.

Something on her arm glinted in the sun as she tucked in one last daisy. Was that her *diamond bracelet*, presented to her by her sons last year when she turned eighty? She loved to show it off when I'd take her to the movies or the steak house. But to work out in the garden? That was odd. It caught the light again as she held her hand up in a wave.

I turned to see a familiar gray Impala come slowly down the street with a rattle I'd heard often in the parking lot at work.

Bill Butterick. What was he doing here? Bill lived three streets over, and he had no reason to be driving by my house.

He rolled his window down and called out to Frances. "Absolutely tragic! In the prime of her life!" With his round face and rotund figure, he seemed to be squeezed into the car; an SUV, I thought, would be more his style.

Frances crossed her arms. "I wish I could be the one to mete out some justice to the imbecile who took her from this world." Frances's face was red as she approached Bill's car. "I would drag that fool by the hairs on his worthless head to somewhere very hot." Then her voice turned soft. "Hannah was a fine girl—like a daughter to me."

I smiled to myself. I'd heard so many compliments ever since the day that I woke up dead.

"Of course," Frances added, "I don't have a clue how she managed to get by, as forgetful as she was. Thank goodness that I had an extra key for all the times she locked herself out of the house." Frances shook her head. "Sweet but scatterbrained. Like a child almost."

What? This was from a woman who had started to lose words for familiar things like "phone" and "laxatives" and "car." There were even times she forgot my name. In turn I had been "Helen," "Hallie," or more recently just "Hon." She once referred to Cleopatra as "Queen Nefertiti," which made me laugh so hard I gasped when I called Maria Claire.

Bill hopped out of his car, and I took note of the chocolate stains all down his shirt. "Have the cops been by again?" he asked. He was trying to be all casual and stuff, but I could tell he was nervous by the way his foot would not be still.

Scott always told me perpetrators liked to keep abreast of investigations. They liked to hang around the places associated with their victims—although I would have guessed they'd have preferred to stay away.

Scott and I had watched a lot of true-crime docs in the Yellow House. I'd become addicted to them in a way, especially with the expert commentary coming from the seat next to me.

"What do you hear?" asked Bill.

Frances shrugged. "They'll tell us when they tell us, Bill. I can report, however, they've been by the house a lot." When Frances wasn't gardening, she was watching out the window. "Hopefully, they're getting close," she told him. "May the poor girl rest in peace."

Bill furrowed his brow in concentration. As usual, there were doughnut crumbs sprinkled in his mustache and all down his shirt, which was a very tight fit on his rotund frame. "They've been out back?" he asked. "Checked behind her house and all?"

Frances glared at him. "Do I look like Sherlock

Holmes? Or like a poor old woman who'd like to be left in peace *in my own front yard?*"

"Well, I will be off, then. I'll just take a little look-see at Hannah's meter first." Bill coughed nervously and brushed some crumbs from his shirt. "I've taken on a side job. Just part-time, of course, until business picks back up." His face lit up in a smile. "Big changes coming soon to Doughnut Delights and More!" He'd been saying that for years, and yet the store with its old décor seemed to be trapped forever in the 1990s.

As I watched him stumble down the side path, careful to avoid the prickly bushes, I remembered something from the week before I died. How had I not thought of it before? That it might be related somehow to my—I could barely think the words—my *murder?*

I had been awakened in the night by the sound of someone outside my window. Mildly alarmed but sleepy, I'd turned on the light and peered out. I had my cell in hand, ready to call Scott at any sign that I had heard a person rather than a stray cat or a branch rustling in the wind.

I could see nothing in the darkness, but I was almost certain I heard footsteps. *Very close.* But if someone was out there, they must have seen the light come on. The sound that I heard was of the footsteps getting further from the house, scurrying away.

Minutes later, I had convinced myself it was dogs or squirrels, the wind. I soon settled back into a dreamless sleep.

Scott had not been happy when I'd told him the next day. "Hannah, I'm a cop," he'd said. "You know I would have come. Someone at your window in the *dead of night?*"

But the footsteps had been *retreating,* and I had been so tired. All I'd wanted was some sleep. Besides, this was Colby Pointe, where nothing ever happened.

Well, until it did.

Now, I followed Bill, who—just as I expected—lumbered past the meter without so much as a glance. He stopped beneath the *very window* where I had heard *the noise.* Then he looked around, a wild look in his eyes. He crawled beneath the bushes and emerged with the big gold watch I'd often seen him wear.

"My father's watch," he'd told me. "Presented to him by *his* father on the occasion of his graduation from the school of dentistry. People nowadays fail to understand how to appreciate a finely crafted watch."

Now he closed his eyes and sighed before he stuffed the watch into his pocket and trudged toward the street, sweating from the effort. Once Frances was in sight, he pasted on the smile that often meant, "Would you like to add a coffee to your order or make that a *three-pack* of delights?"

"All done here!" he said. He gave a small wave to Frances, who had moved into *my* yard to do some weeding.

She nodded silently to him and went back into her house, closing the door behind her. My heart fell a little when I saw that her diamond bracelet had landed on the sidewalk near a tree.

I stared at Bill, who had reached up to mop his brow with his handkerchief as he walked to his car. Now I *had* to find a way to make Scott understand I knew important things. Had Bill meant to kill me at my home that night? If so, why had he run instead of finishing the job? And over a downturn in his business—a business that, let's face it, had been slowly dying for ten years?

I was missing something here.

Now, Bill looked down in shock at the gleaming stream of diamonds. "Her bracelet!" he whispered. He picked it up and peered at the jewelry in his hand. "Very, very nice."

Don't you do it, Bill.

With a look of alarm, he rushed to Frances's house and held the bracelet out to her when she opened her door just a crack.

"Well, now, why do you have *that?*" she said by way of thank you, slamming the door in his face.

I sunk down on my front stoop, thinking hard. Was Bill desperate enough for money to kill the competition—and yet honest enough not to pocket an old lady's string of diamonds? It would have been so easy for him to slip that bracelet in his pocket for himself.

I remembered some wise words from my mailman, of all people. "People aren't just one thing; they are many, Hannah. Every day in different moments, each one of us is a saint, a thief, a fool. When I feel anger toward a man, I remind myself that a person is much more than a moment. He is much more than the moment he cuts in front of me in line—or takes the curve too fast at First and Elm and almost wipes me out."

But what about murder, Toby? That is a whole different kind of man.

On our cul-de-sac, the resident guru wore a uniform and carried a mailbag. But I doubted even Toby Sykes could give me any answers now for all the questions swirling in my head.

Andi came around the curve just then with Cleopatra. As usual, she looked like a fashion plate, with white capris and a pink top that was a perfect match for the pink flats on her feet. My blonde and tiny neighbor had even matched her outfit to the dog's. Cleopatra was now proudly sporting a bandanna with the words "Good Girl" spelled out in tiny pink paw prints. The dog, I was glad to see, was full of energy and spirit. But as the pair got closer to me, the big dog sniffed the air and whimpered; she seemed to be confused.

Andi paused to rub Cleopatra's side. "Do you recognize your old house?" she asked Cleopatra gently. "Are you confused, sweet girl?"

I threw a cheese treat from my pocket, and Cleopatra joyfully ate it up. *Good, good girl,* I thought, tossing her another.

"Where did..." Andi looked around and frowned. "Is it, like, *raining cheese?*" She tugged gently on the leash. "Let's go say hello to Frances."

My neighbor had ambled back into her yard to water her Bougainvillea. "Keep that dog away from my plants now, Andi," Frances said.

"Oh, she doesn't want *a flower* when dog treats just seemingly *appear* from the sky." Andi thought about that some more then shrugged. "It just breaks my heart, walking by this house. Hannah should be here!" Then a sad smile crossed her face as if she remembered something. "No one could tell a story or make you laugh the way that Hannah could."

Frances sniffed. "Well, I'm glad she made you laugh, but Hannah was a horror. Lots of trouble, that one."

What? What had happened to "like a daughter to me, sweet but scatterbrained?"

Andi stared, wide-eyed. "Frances, you don't mean it."

Cleopatra growled at Frances.

Frances moved with her can of water to a line of tiny purple buds. She nodded toward my house. "Did you know the woman who lived in that house right there *stole a check out of my mailbox?* How can an old woman afford to pay her bills with all that going on?"

"Frances," Andi told her gently, "I think you must be confused."

"And did you know last year she stole my *Christmas gifts?* Right out of my car, she did! Trouble, trouble, trouble. I was watching out my window when she did it. I saw it as clear as day. Should have smacked her with my broom." A smile spread across her face. "That would have felt real good."

This was *not* the Frances that I knew.

Andi cocked her head. "Frances, that was *Heather*, who took your Christmas presents. They arrested *Heather*, who lived down the street. Don't you remember now? How Heather and her family had…well, financial complications." She looked hard at Frances. "*Hannah* was the one who looked out for you. *Hannah* lived next door in that house right there." She tilted her head to the right. "Hannah gave you rides. Hannah was your friend."

Frances looked startled then confused then angry. "Isn't that what I just said?" she spat. "*Hannah* was a good one, but that *Heather?* What a mess!" Then she glared at Andi. "Why are you standing there? Can't you tell that I am busy making sure these plants don't die?"

"I won't keep you from your gardening," Andi said, concerned, "but if you need me, Frances, call."

"And you do the same, dear. Oh, and by the way, that necklace you have on looks kind of pricey, so a word to the wise." She turned toward my house. "The woman who lives there loves to take things for herself that *do not* belong to her. Heather is her name. Or maybe it is Heloise or Helen. Someone with an *H*."

CHAPTER THREE

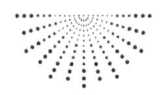

That night I couldn't sleep, so I made my way out to the side porch to look up at the stars. It was what I liked to do when I had things to figure out.

Celeste appeared across from me in the chair where Scott sometimes liked to sit. She looked up as well. "It's nice up there, you know," she told me quietly. "The stars are brighter up close, and Hannah, you can touch them. You can hold a million stars at once! It's like all the glitter in the world slipping through your fingers." She looked at me gently. "I know you loved your life, but the next world will enchant you. You have my promise, Hannah." A dreamy smile spread across her face, and I wondered if that world was fairly new to her as well.

"Soon. I'll go with you soon." I settled back against

the cushions of my chair, fighting off the tears. I missed the warmth of Cleopatra pressed up against my side.

"You know, the supervisors are all up in arms about this crazy glitch," Celeste said thoughtfully. "They have no idea how it happened—that Scott could *talk to you*. The investigation has been moved up—way up in the ranks." A look of worry crossed her face. "So much of the universe depends on the separation of our world and theirs. So it is crucial, Hannah, you stay away from Scott." She gave me a look. "Do you understand?"

Stay away? No way.

"Well, I can see that you're verklempt," Celeste said in a whisper before she disappeared. "I'll give you time alone."

But I was not alone for long. Even from a distance, I could recognize the energetic strides.

Toby! I lifted my hand in a wave—until the awful truth hit me once again: *He cannot see you, Hannah.* Life was lonely as a ghost.

If anyone could help me find a sense of peace, it would be the man walking toward me now. Our mailman's eyes, encased in a sea of wrinkles, held a lot of wisdom; they had seen a lot of things. It was because of advice from Toby that I'd done a lot of things. I'd applied for the promotion and taken weekend trips with Scott without fretting over cost. I'd stayed up too late with

Andi to solve the problems of the world from my little porch. Toby taught me to be brave enough to say *yes* to all the things. Thank goodness that he had, since neither of us knew my time would be so short.

But what in the world was Toby doing out at this time of night? Exercise perhaps? A former executive from Wall Street, he'd taken the walking route after he retired last May. "To breathe in the fresh air and stretch my legs and get to know my neighbors," he'd explained the first time we met.

I'd often see him working late—or early—to get in his deliveries and still enjoy a full slate of retirement pleasures. Toby was known to play an excellent game of golf and to enjoy a fine whiskey with his drinking club out on the waterfront. He was a frequent guest at the Yellow House as well, often buying tickets for a double feature and discussing films with me over coffees or desserts.

I watched him stop at Frances's, maybe with that check, which would make her sorry she'd accused me— and right before I died. That is, if she *remembered* I was dead—or that I was her neighbor Hannah.

As my friendly mailman disappeared around the corner, I stood up and stretched. Then, still feeling restless, I took a walk around the house.

It was getting close to midnight, and I could hear

Scott now. Scott was a worrier, which I found kind of cute. It was like he wanted to lock me in a box to make sure I stayed safe. *What are you doing, Hannah?* he would say. *It's the middle of the night. We've had reports of prowlers, and then there was that person right there at your window.*

Hey, but I was dead. What more could happen to me now?

As I made my way to the front, I saw a familiar bulky figure sitting on the steps.

Scott. My heart swelled at the sight of that one curl that always fell into his eyes.

"I couldn't keep you safe," he said, as if speaking to the slight breeze that was stirring in the trees. "At the most important thing in my whole life, I failed."

I longed to tell him no, that it was not his fault.

I took a seat beside him, breathing in his familiar, woodsy scent. "Hey." I spoke very softly. It might be less startling that way.

Instead of jumping up this time, he gazed into my face as his eyes filled up with tears. "What is happening?" he whispered. "Have I lost my mind?"

"It's me!" I held his hand. "Scott, I'm really here. For some reason, through some celestial quirk, I have some extra time. Please believe me, Scott." I put my arm through his. "I don't understand a lot about what is happening here. But I really miss you. And I promise that I'm real."

He ran a hand down my cheek and gently through my hair. "You *feel* real," he whispered. "Hannah! You feel *alive*."

"I *want* to be alive." Tears were threatening again, but this was my time to be strong. I had to savor every second of this bonus time I got to spend with Scott. I had to help him solve my murder. And we had to solve it quick, because at any minute Celeste could swoop right in and yank me away from Scott.

Tears were rolling down his cheeks, which pulled so hard at my heart. I had never seen him cry.

"Can't you just stay with me?" he asked in an almost pleading tone. "If you're here, and I'm here, can't we just stay like this?"

"I don't have long, they say." I lay my head against his shoulder, and he buried his head in my hair.

"You still smell like you," he whispered.

I lifted my face for a kiss, and that felt real as well.

"Who killed me, Scott? Who did it?" I asked after a while.

"They've assigned the case to Rick." He let out a sigh. "It's routine that those of us closest to the victim cannot get too involved."

Rick Trimble was the one who was supposed to catch

my killer? This just got worse and worse.

"Ah, I know," said Scott, who could always read my mind. "But believe me, Hannah, all hands are on deck. The chief is working day and night on this thing as well, as is every cop we have. This guy is going down." A darkness moved across his face.

"Suspects?" I dared to ask.

"Rick believes that it was a random...killing." Scott could hardly say the word. "With the intent of theft. He is thinking maybe it was someone passing through, not somebody here in town. It was an out-of-towner, though, that will make our job a lot more complicated."

Rick was way off track, according to my ghostly intuition, if that was a thing.

"So, you didn't *see* him, Hannah?" Scott looked into my eyes. "Did he say anything at all? Tell me what you know."

"It happened all so fast. I never turned around. I never saw his face." There had been no time to react between the footsteps—getting closer, closer—and the nightmarish feel of that squeezing on my throat.

"But I have things to tell you." I grabbed his hands in both of mine. I began with Frances and her furor at me, along with the fact that she had me confused with Heather and thought I had stolen from her. "She is *all* worked up."

"You've talked to Frances since you died?"

"Oh, no. Only you can see me, and that's not supposed to happen."

Then Scott began to think out loud about a plan. "We'll check Frances out for sure—and both her sons as well," he said. "Ed plays softball with us, and the guy can be a hothead." He paused to think a moment. "We have talked to Frances several times already, and it will be routine to go back and check in with her again—as your closest neighbor. But to bring in Ed and Les, we'd need some kind of evidence to compel them to come in. What would I list as a reason? Crucial information, as provided to me by a ghost?"

"Just tell me where to find them, and I'll hang around and watch," I said. "I'm invisible! It can be a superpower when it comes to surveillance."

"We do have some prints," said Scott thoughtfully, "from the shopping bag you dropped. There was a receipt inside that matched your credit card, so we know that it was yours. That could be a help if we come up with a suspect who's legit—and if the prints turn out to be a match."

"Try Bill Butterick," I said.

"The guy who sells the doughnuts?" Scott raised an eyebrow at me.

"He might have killed me, Scott."

It turned out that Scott already knew about the confrontation at the movie house. Not surprisingly, some witnesses had come forward with the story after I was killed.

"He's just a sad, sad guy," said Scott. "Divorced three times and kind of a loner. He's known to blow off steam, but they don't think he's the guy."

"Oh, there's more," I said. I told Scott about the "meter check" and the watch that Bill had pulled out from behind the bushes. "I guess it was him that night when I heard someone prowling at my place."

Now, Scott's face was red with fury. "I have a mind to just skip the arrest and exact some punishment of my own creation. Jail is way too comfortable for a guy like that." Then he closed his eyes until his breaths grew even. "That's good information, Hannah. Very useful stuff. I just need a way to tell the chief how I know what I know." He sat quietly with his thoughts. "To say there's no precedent for this is an understatement."

I heard the familiar night sounds; an owl and a whip-poor-will; perhaps they had come to say goodbye as well. I snuggled close to Scott. I wondered if we would have married or had children, how long our time together could have stretched. I would have to settle for a few more days—or even hours maybe.

I jumped up from the steps; there was no time to

waste. I had that pressing list of important one-more-times.

"I would like an ice cream," I announced to Scott. "That strawberry-shortcake flavor with chocolate bits and sprinkles." I grabbed his hand to pull him up. "Kay's Ice Cream Shoppe! Let's go!"

A look of sadness crossed his eyes. "Oh, Hannah. Please believe that I would go out and buy you all the ice cream in the world. But no way is that place open in the middle of the night."

I raised a playful eyebrow. "It's one of my superpowers to slip in and out of any place I want. Just give me your order, and we will take our cones and eat them in the park. Look how bright the moon is. It will be perfect, Scott."

He stood up and softly kissed me. "Let's go, then. It's a date!" Then his forehead wrinkled.

"What's the matter now?" I asked.

"Well, technically, you see, that would be a break-and-enter, and as a member of law enforcement in this city, I cannot condone…"

I held up a hand. "I will leave a fifty, so they'll profit from the deal." What would be the use of saving money now? I could give them all the money I had in the world for two ice cream cones! "It will be a win-win," I told my handsome cop.

CHAPTER FOUR

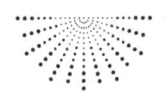

We enjoyed our ice cream. (Triple scoop for me—time was running short.) Then after we were finished, we didn't want to leave. It was way too nice outside, so we walked around the park.

Why had we never done this: a walk in Hanson Park in the middle of the night! It was a whole new place under the dim street lamps while the rest of the town slept.

"We should have done this more," he told me softly, as if he had read my mind. He kissed the top of my head. "Shame on you," he teased. "You got me to try crazy foods and to go upside down on that Whoopsie-Daisy ride. But you never told me how really nice this was, walking in the park in the middle of the night." He pulled me a little closer as we continued down the path.

"I never thought to try it, and I thought there was time." I tried very hard to keep the tears out of my voice.

The glow from the moonlight and the street lamps painted a gold and white mosaic pattern in the lake. In the stillness, I could hear everything: Scott's slow and even breathing, the wind rustling in the trees, an owl calling to another in the distant pines across the park.

And then...*what was that noise?* Very clearly, I could hear the sound of footsteps getting closer.

"Who is that?" I whispered, stopping short and holding tightly to Scott's arm.

He quickly pulled me to him, as if he could protect me, as if I were a girl (I wished!) who could still be saved. Then I gasped. "It's him!"

As the figure grew closer in the shadows, I recognized Bill's rounded belly and his slow and labored gait. There was something in his hand—something large and square.

"It's Bill!" I turned away from Scott to get a closer look, but I could feel the fury rising in him.

"That worthless excuse for a—" he fumed.

"Scott, you need to hide!" I interrupted, a plan quickly forming in my mind. Like a fool, I *whispered,* although I remembered quickly that I could shout the words and no one would hear but Scott. I was still getting used to my altered state.

"Behind that bush—or *somewhere*," I continued, switching to my normal voice. "I will follow Bill! Then I'll come back and report."

While Scott ducked behind a clump of trees, I set out behind my target, who was moving slowly—an easy man to follow. In his hand, I now could see, was a taped-up cardboard box. His steps seemed to grow even slower as we moved past the mermaid statue and then around the corner. Then we continued past the playground, where a stray breeze had begun to gently rock the swings.

Toward the east end of the park, he stopped by a large magnolia. Huffing from the walk, he set down the box, then he squeezed his heavy body into a thick stand of bushes—where he disappeared for quite a while. I watched the bushes shake with whatever flurry of activity was going on in there. *Very, very strange.*

While I waited for him to emerge, I moved closer to the box. On the upper right, printed carefully in thick black pen was a single word—or name.

"Saudade?" Who in the world was that? Or was it a thing? Or place? Was it Saudade's stuff that was packed up in the box? Was she part of the reason he had wanted me to die—if it had indeed been Bill who strangled me that night? That did not seem right. What had I ever done to someone named Saudade?

As I pondered all of that, he emerged at last with a

rusty shovel, which I supposed he had hidden earlier for his little mission. He wiped some sweat from his brow, and then he got to work digging a hole beneath the tree a little larger than the box. Then I watched, impatient, as he lowered the box into the shallow hole and piled the dirt back on, taking the time to almost lovingly spread the dirt across its new resting place.

Just get on with it, I thought, *and get out of here so I can see what's in that box.* That thing was getting pulled out of the ground just as soon as he was gone. I had a feeling the contents of the box might hold the answer to two burning questions: not only *who* but *why.*

The thing about it was, though, this guy wouldn't leave. Instead, I had to wait while he sat there on the ground and sobbed. Finally, all cried out at last, he gently touched the dirt above the box. "It could have been stupendous," he said softly, as if speaking to the ground. "Ah, yes—a fine, fine thing." Then finally he stood. He looked down at the shovel. "Ah, who needs the thing?" he said morosely before walking off without it.

That someone would be me! I would need the shovel! But first I ran to Scott to let him know what was going on; I knew Scott was anxious too. The first thing that I did was put my fingers to my lips to let him know he was not to come out of hiding yet. "That cardboard box!" I almost shouted. "He buried it beneath a tree. And he left a shovel! For us to dig it up."

But first I had to make sure Bill was really out of there and would not be coming back to check on something he'd forgotten. I ran back to watch his progress. I wasn't doing anything until I saw with my two eyes his Impala on the road back to town. Bill could not see me, but he *could* see, I imagined, dirt being shoveled from the ground and his cardboard box emerging.

It soon became apparent his departure was going to take a while. He was trudging up a hill in almost the same spot I had left him when I ran to Scott. I sunk down on a bench and watched as he stopped several times, red-faced, to lean down, hands on his knees, to catch his breath.

It was *not* that big of a hill.

It is unfortunate to be anxious—and in relatively good shape—when the person you are spying on is very fond of doughnuts and not so fond of exercise.

I walked back to report again to Scott since it seemed it would be a while before Bill's Impala rolled out of the lot. I told him about Bill's behavior and what was written on the box. Then we fell silent as we waited, and I found myself, again, choked up. At the end of this little quest, I might finally learn the reason I had *died*. It was a sobering thought.

"You did great work, Hannah," Scott whispered soothingly. "I'm proud of you for that."

I leaned back against him as he gently ran his fingers through my hair. I closed my eyes and tried to be as patient as I could, breathing in Scott's familiar scent and feeling his warmth against me.

A couple of times he shook his head when I tried to pull him up to run and grab the shovel. "Not just yet," he told me quietly. "Bill strikes me as the type to find a reason to double back for something he forgot. To remember that his car is at the west gate, not the east." He let out a heavy sigh. "Surveillance is...well, it's not as *action-packed* as the movies make it seem."

I sighed and closed my eyes. When I opened them again, he was staring at me. "Are you sure that you can't stay? Please don't leave me, Hannah." It came out like a plea.

My answer was a kiss, which I wanted to go on, knowing it might be the last one—ever! Who knew how long it would be before they made me leave. I suddenly decided that the box could wait. The reason that I *died* now seemed less important than the reason I was so desperate to *stay*. I pressed in closer to him and put my hand on his cheek as our kiss grew deeper.

That's when things got strange.

At that very moment, the wind picked up like crazy;

the air turned strangely cold, and a familiar voice cried out, "No, no, no, no!" Then I felt an arm jerk me away from Scott, and I was nose to nose with Celeste behind a different line of bushes.

"What did I tell you, Hannah?" Celeste's eyes were wide. "No talking to the living! I thought I made that clear."

I pulled away from her, feeling furious and guilty all at once. "I wasn't...*talking* to him at the moment."

"*That* is forbidden most of all. Don't you see that kissing would be even worse?" She crossed her arms to study me. "Already, you are so enamored with him that your soul will not cross over to the other side. The idea is to *let go* of the things you love on earth, not the opposite."

"I know. It's just hard. Would it hurt for me to have just a few more minutes?"

"Yes, Hannah. Possibly, it could."

I breathed in deeply as I took that in: I might not speak to Scott again. "Five minutes wouldn't hurt," I said under my breath. "Just to say goodbye."

Celeste rubbed at her nails, which today were white with flecks of chartreuse glitter. "I'm not the enemy, you know." She sounded almost pouty. "I don't make the rules." She looked up from her nails to me. "He does seem perfect for you. I can see that, Hannah, and I am at heart a big romantic. It's not like I am here as some *enemy of love!*"

"Oh, I don't think that," I said.

"Back when I was living, do you know what I would *always* read out on the beach? I would read romances! Every single time." She let out a sigh. "But I also know that this system failure—or whatever is happening with you—could have major consequences."

My chest tightened up. "Celeste, what have you heard?"

"They don't tell me much. Low-level newbie here! But I have heard some things. And I have to tell you that I'm scared."

In the distance, I heard Scott and peeked out at him from the bushes.

He turned in circles, looking around him wildly. "Hannah! What the…" He was so far away. Celeste, it seemed, had whisked me way across the park.

Nervously, she twirled a long curl. "I heard one of the bosses tell another that the future of the world is dependent on that line between *us* and *them* not being penetrated. There are things that have to happen for mankind to survive—things that were set in place before the dinosaurs, the cavemen, all of that. If spirits start to break through, interact with humans—and recast the course of events—who knows what can happen!"

Spending time with Scott hardly seemed the kind of thing to change the future of the world. Still, a feeling of unease had settled in my stomach.

"Hannah!" Scott was walking quickly down the pathway, searching.

Celeste pulled me further out of sight. "No one has ever seen this kind of thing before," she said. "The bosses are afraid that your interactions here might summon other spirits who might attempt to do the same. And, believe you me, there are some of them who want to do just that. Some of them are itching to undo the progress being made to protect the water and the air. They want to stir up wars! Some of them were taken to the other side for specific reasons," she told me in a hushed voice, "and they might be the very ones to make contact with the living if they could. Their *power* is the thing they could not let go of from their time on earth." She sank down on the ground. "Why do I always get the complicated cases?" She crossed her arms and frowned. "I thought I was very clear on what had to happen. I thought I could trust you, Hannah!"

"I'll behave," I told her. Although it would be hard. "I didn't understand that the situation was so...dire. I don't want to be the one to cause any kind of war!"

Had I just said that sentence? Had she really said that

—"war"? I sat down beside her. "Could that happen? Really?"

She shrugged. "I just know that the bosses are concerned. They don't really know how far things could go if the word gets out that *one of us* can speak to *one of them*."

"So your bosses think I could be sending out some signal to the others to say, 'Hey, come on down?'"

"Oh, some of the other spirits—way too many of them—are already here. You are not the first to dig your heels in, Hannah, and refuse to go," she said. "But they cannot *interact*, like you did with Scott. That's what makes you different—and why the higher-ups are all over me like cotton candy on a cloud."

"*Wait.* Clouds are made of...? Oh, just never mind."

"The fact that you can *talk* to Scott means there's something we have not detected, a weakness in the system." Celeste ran a hand through her hair, wrinkling her nose as she frowned. "There are others we've been watching who have stuck around like you. Some of them are just well-meaning spirits who don't want to leave their people. Or their lives or their dogs. But there are evil ones as well, just itching to continue what they did on earth." She shuddered. "Really awful things." She looked me in the eye. "Like, *cataclysmic* things."

Well, this was not my vision of the afterlife. "What kind of things?" I asked.

She watched me carefully then seemed to come to a decision. She stood up and grabbed my hand. "Come away with me."

Things went dark for just a second—dark with silver sparkles—then we were in the lobby at the Yellow House. It was closed up for the night, of course, but we could see well enough in the dim lighting that we kept on overnight.

Celeste took my hand and led me to a poster for a documentary coming in two weeks about the worst dictators in the nation's history. *D is for Diabolical* had gotten lots of buzz, and we had a history professor coming in to speak on opening night.

"Imagine," said Celeste, "that some of history's worst monsters have come back to the earth. That they refuse to leave—like you."

I stared at her, appalled.

"These are just the types most keen to find a way to do the thing you've done: to influence the living to take certain actions, to be heard and seen by living people. Of course, we have always thought there was no way that could happen. And then there was you." She sighed and gave me a look—which just wasn't fair.

"Not my fault!" I held up my hands. "I can't help the

fact that I woke up dead but *somehow still right here*—instead of in that other place."

Then, to my surprise, my Guide began to cry. "I can't help but wonder if it's all *my* fault!" she said. "Did I do something wrong when you first transitioned?" Then she composed herself. "I know you're not to blame. Sorry to be snippy. It's just that they're going nuts up there in the High Offices. And they are blaming *me* that Scott can interact with you. So much pressure, Hannah!" She took a calming breath. "There are certain spirits that we have been watching for quite a while at this point. People who were taken from the world in the midst of plotting any number of atrocities to the human race. What they'd love to do is not be foiled by death, to whisper evil plans into the ears of those who can carry out the missions that were cut short when they died. If they catch on to the fact that *you* have bucked the system, they may try to study you. They may try to find a way to take on for themselves the powers that you have."

"But even I don't understand how I am doing it," I said.

"Well, we need to figure that out before these evil spirits do." She collapsed onto a bench. "I told them all along I was a better fit for something else—Spirit Fashion maybe. Or Hue Selector for the Department of

Sunrises and Sunsets. Not something super brainy like a Guide. I am more artistic and more fashion-forward than I am an analyzer of complicated things." She thought for a while as she crossed her legs and jiggled one chartreuse high heel. After a while, she posed a question. "What do you know, Hannah, about the history of this place?" She gazed around at the movie house.

I sat down beside her. "Do you think that all of this might have some connection to the Yellow House?"

"It's significant, I think, that the movie house is where your power first emerged. I feel something odd here. It's like a kind of energy I've never felt before."

I thought back on the few facts I'd been told. "It was built in 2004," I said. "It's always been a movie house." I would have thought a "haunted" place might be super old with some kind of gruesome history, but who was I to say?

"Hmm," Celeste replied. "There must be *something* in its history." She sat and thought some more before leaping up. "Well, I should get you to the park. Guides are not to interfere in the location of the spirits in their care. So it was against the rules to use the Angel Transport to bring you on this little ride. But I can be a rebel too." She gave me a wink.

Then things went dark again—this time with

turquoise sparkles—and we were at the park behind the same line of bushes.

I peeked from behind the leaves to see Scott stretched out on the ground, his focus on the sky. That was what both of us liked to do when we needed calming down: lie flat and look up at the stars. "These blessed candles of the night," was what Scott liked to call them.

Doesn't that just show you why I couldn't go? How could you not love a Shakespeare-quoting cop?

"Scott will be okay," Celeste told me quietly. She paused for a moment. "Hey, look, I get it, Hannah. Do you think you're the only one who's ever felt these things? Very few of us were okay with having to move on when—out of nowhere, big surprise—it was our turn to go."

I paused, a question in my eye.

She looked down at the ground before she met my eye. "I died on my honeymoon," she said. "Two years ago last month. I also had a Scott. But this is dangerous. It has to stop. Right now."

"I get what you're saying." Which meant I would *try*. But I knew Celeste was right; I had to do more than try. This was bigger than just me. I glanced at Celeste, who had begun to shake. "Are you okay?" I asked.

"It's just a lot," she said. "This is my first month

without a supervisor, and you are one of *eight* I'm supposed to help. And later on tonight, I am scheduled to stand by at an *explosion.* Four brand-new assignees. So much for eternal rest."

Then I became distracted by police lights in the distance. As the car got closer, the driver killed the lights and pulled to a stop—close enough to keep an eye on Scott, but not close enough for Scott to notice.

Was it Rick inside the car? Was Rick there tailing Scott?

"Is Scott in danger too?" My voice was hushed as I turned to Celeste.

A shadow crossed her face. "What you don't find out in this life, you are not *meant* to know," she answered. "It messes with the balance, throws things all out of order."

Then I turned back to Scott, who now was sitting up with his head in his hands.

Celeste's voice turned gentle. "The two of you will be together in another life." She put her hand on my arm. "This is not the end."

"But by then, Scott might be someone else's husband."

"That's a label for your world, not for ours."

When Scott got up and walked away, I noticed the police car followed at a distance.

After a little while, Celeste pulled me toward the exit

in the opposite direction from the path that Scott had taken, leading me toward home. "Did I tell you about our trees?" she asked me softly as we walked underneath a canopy of green. "Leaves in every color—silver, pink, and purple. So soft to the touch."

"Celeste, I really want to know who killed me. Can I get just a hint?"

"Focus on the next world. Look ahead, not back." She said it with the enthusiasm of a mid-level manager who was reciting jargon she'd been trained to say. "The goings-on in this world are no longer yours to know." Then she paused and frowned. "Although, I have to say…I would be glad to leave a place where a person acts like a friend by day and…oh, it was awful, Hannah, how you had to die."

So I had been right: I was murdered by a "friend."

CHAPTER FIVE

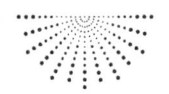

I couldn't sleep—again. And how *could* I sleep? Celeste had made it sound like the whole world could erupt into chaos if I did not behave. For the first time, I wished I could just move on to that other world. But I did not know how. I just knew until it happened, I had to stay away from Scott lest the world implode. In my mind, I saw him at the park, so broken up by my disappearance.

And we'd come *so close* to a major clue about what was up with Bill.

Which was reason two why I couldn't sleep. The answer to my burning questions could be buried at that moment under a magnolia in the park. Maybe if I knew who had strangled me that night and why, things inside me could feel settled. Then I could move on to the next place, and the world would once again be safe.

As sometimes happened when I was at a loss, words of wisdom from a postman floated to the surface of my thoughts. "The answer to your problem may be simpler than you think," Toby had told me once. I had been complaining about how much I had to spend to feed my appetite for biographies and mysteries, which I always liked to stay up too late to read.

"Have you ever heard of the Colby Pointe Library?" asked Toby teasingly. "The most amazing thing! Books are absolutely free."

Simpler than you think. A plan began to form. Celeste had been specific: no talking to or kissing Scott. Celeste had never told me I could not dig up a box.

Which is how I found myself back in the park that night, a shovel in my hand. Celeste might not approve, but she had her hands full that night with her explosion. Celeste would never know.

With a little effort, I managed to dig up the hole and pull the box out of the ground. After I pulled off the tape and pulled apart the lid, I was met with the sight of a lot of tissue. I was struck right away by how carefully each of the objects had been wrapped. I settled down, cross-legged, by the box and took a breath for courage.

First, I unwrapped a single mitten. It was red with

white snowflakes embroidered down the center. Next was a lime green rubber duck with a daisy painted on his back.

I had no idea what I was expecting, but this wasn't it. *This* was not telling me a story about why I had to die.

I unwrapped more tissue to uncover a pair of tiger ears like a kid might wear for fun. I sighed, disappointed. Had Bill lost his mind? If so, that might bump him up a little higher on the "likely killer" list.

The rest of the box was filled with gorgeous hand-carved pieces for a chess set with a *Star Wars* theme.

Had these perhaps belonged to "Saudade," if that was, in fact, a name? French perhaps or Spanish?

Then I caught sight of a folded piece of paper in the bottom of the box. I reached for it carefully. Someone (Bill?) had written, "Goodbye, Goodbye, Goodbye…" a zillion times in a neat cursive hand all up and down the page.

I felt a chill run through me. Should this "Saudade" be warned?

I took out my cell and shot a picture of the box so I would have the name. Then I took photos of the items one by one before taping the box up and covering it back up with dirt. I put the shovel back into its place in the bushes. All was back as I found it, very little "interfering" done, but I was more confused than ever.

The next day, I slept in. I drank a cup of coffee, feeling lonelier than ever. With the stay-away-from-Scott rule, there was no one to talk things over with, no one to ask, "How was your day?"

My eyes were drawn to Cleopatra's stuffed blue dragon in the corner. I wished I could have kept my dog at least—since "dead" apparently translated to "still here." But while I could set out food, the sweet pug could no longer feel my cuddles or my tummy rubs. Cleopatra needed Andi. I was happy she was being pampered and that she was only down the street. That would have to be enough.

Soon I wandered outside when I looked out my window and saw Frances working in her yard. Today she had managed to wear matching socks, but she had on one yellow gardening glove—along with one red mitten.

I did a double take. The mitten matched the one that Bill had buried.

My heart rate shot up like a rocket. What could the connection be between Bill and Frances? She had been gruff with Bill, didn't seem to have much use for him at all. But then again, Frances found some reason to complain about almost everyone she met.

I took three deep breaths. I'd watch Frances for a while then head over to the doughnut shop to keep an eye on Bill. Also on my list was to figure out where Rick might be on patrol that day.

But first I simply wanted to take some time to study the intricate ways that white intertwined with red in the delicate small blooms in my neighbor's yard. Two opposite emotions seemed to be warring in me. The need to rush to find my killer was at odds with the little voice that said to…well, to "smell the roses" while I could. I seemed to notice everything since I had been dead—like the way the flowers in Frances's large garden moved from shades of dark to light.

I sat down beside her, choosing a patch of ground in the sun. Then I watched her working carefully to dig some holes, adding compost to them before putting in the blooms. She had always told me that she'd teach me, but I was too busy, which struck me now as wrong, as Frances was a master gardener. I took mental notes as she made sure each plant had lots of space to grow.

She'd already put in some purple ones, and there were some left over, sitting on her porch. She had always told me that she bought too much. "I was never good at math," she'd say. "You take some of those next door."

But I was too busy, and what kind of life was that?

Too busy just to dig a simple hole and put some flowers in it? Well, now I seemed to have some time. I took the flowers from the porch and began to plant. I borrowed compost too; Frances wouldn't mind.

That's what I was doing when Toby made his way down the street. "Best yard on the block," he called as he winked at my neighbor.

She gave him the evil eye. "You got that check I'm missing?"

Toby rifled through his bag. "Just some coupons from the grocery and two magazines." He stared down at the top one. "This one here claims to have 'Five Exciting Twists for Cupcakes that Will Wow.' I will expect a little taste if you give that a try."

She got up slowly from the ground. "You still don't have my check, and now you're asking me to *make you some dessert?* That check belongs to me! Now, you tell me where it is right now."

Toby put her mail in the box then held up both his hands. "I am just the mailman! All I do is deliver what they give me to hand out."

Her eyes got narrower as she looked in the distance. "I think that woman took it." She pointed a bony finger straight ahead. "She walks past my house all the time."

I followed her gaze to where Andi was walking Cleopatra down the cross street. Today, Cleopatra had on a baby blue bandanna and Andi wore a jogging suit in a matching shade.

"Andi? That's not right!" said Toby. "Andi is a fine girl, as honest as they come."

Frances grumbled to herself as she kneeled back down and got back to her planting.

Toby walked to my place and pulled some mail out of his bag. "I'm guessing there is someone who is getting Hannah's mail. Don't you want to take these magazines that came for her? I think she would like it if they got some use." He looked down at the cover. "I read this one yesterday. 'The World's Most Haunted Places.' Now, that article right there is just a bunch of nonsense."

Frances scowled again. "So now you don't believe in ghosts? Well, it might just be that *ghosts* don't believe in *mailmen!* How would you like that?"

"Wouldn't hurt my feelings." He put the mail in my box. "So I take it you believe in the paranormal."

"I used to be a skeptic." A proud smile spilled across her face. "Until one fine day at the movies, when I made the acquaintance of none other than Mrs. Lauren Bacall herself!"

"You don't say!" said Toby.

"She was in line behind me for concessions, and I turned around and told her I admired her shoes. She was right there, plain as day, in line for popcorn at the

Yellow House. Asked for her butter very light. Watching her figure, don't you know. Had on the very same fine clothes as in the movie I had a ticket for that day. Very lovely movie with Marilyn Monroe. Why, it was like Ms. Bacall had walked right off the screen." She stood up and put her hands on her hips. "So yes, I myself am a believer."

"And I am as well," said Toby. "When I said to you that the story was a lot of nonsense, I was not implying I do not believe. I was referring to the fact that they left out the Yellow House, which is a very special place when it comes to visits from the other side. I've heard other stories about that movie house. Yours is not the first."

"Oh, yeah?" Frances cocked her head to one side, interested.

"One of my golfing buddies claimed to have had a gin and tonic with Ernest Hemingway last year at the bar. He had just been watching a documentary on the lives of writers. Hemingway, I think, took some issue with some of the things they said, but he liked it overall."

So I was not the first. I was just the first one who got caught by her Guide and the High Office.

Toby rocked back and forth, like he did when he was thinking. "I have long had a theory about the Yellow House," he said.

Frances rolled her eyes. "Is there anything you don't have a theory on?"

"Just think about it for a moment." Toby's eyes were bright. "Where is it you can watch dead people come to life in living color? On a movie screen of course! Which makes the Yellow House the perfect place for them to slip back into the world, have a drink or popcorn, step out into the city if they wish."

"What a bad deal for the ghosts," said Frances with a frown. "Don't you imagine they were hoping for somewhere more exciting? Like Paris or New York? To come back to life in Colby Pointe must be such a disappointment."

Toby thought a moment. "Somewhere at the Yellow House, there must be a crack in whatever *force* keeps the dead on one side and you and me on another," he said carefully. "Oh, I do believe that there are other truly haunted places. But not places where the ghosts just walk up and speak and ask what kind of gin is stocked there in the bar. Thus, my theory of a crack." He leaned up against a tree. "Bacall and Hemingway, you see, come in on reels of film to be projected on a screen. To live again up there! So many of the dead alive again on the screen!" He shrugged. "And some of them, I suppose, decide to stick around to see how the world is faring in these modern times."

I, of course, had not arrived on a reel of film, but if there was indeed a "crack" at the Yellow House, I had found it too. This might make Celeste feel better. The dead and the living had been interacting for a while—and the world was still intact.

"I went to another of her movies too, but Ms. Bacall was a no-show," Frances said. "Very disappointing. I thought we might be friends! She and I are two of a kind, you know. A lot of things in common."

I saw Toby try—somewhat successfully—to hold back a smile.

"Both of us have a reputation for being 'difficult,' but we are both strong women who know what we want. Nothing wrong with that!"

"Oh, no. Not a thing," said Toby.

"And what I want is my check." She put another flower in the ground, then she looked up at Toby. "This business with the mail is simply a disaster. Bill Butterick was telling me just the other day his check was late as well. What is the deal with that? Seems like an easy job to me. Take mail out of the bag, put mail in the box."

"Easy enough, Frances, if the checks have, in fact, been mailed," said Toby. "And you know as well as I do how it is with Bill," he said in a confidential tone. "All pie in the sky with that one. Do you know he told me once that he once had plans to make it big being *on the televi-*

sion? Checks and TV stardom and big doings at the doughnut place—it's all wishful thinking, I'm afraid. Which is just a shame. Seems like a nice guy."

With a grunt, Frances went back to her digging. "He claims he's getting ready to sell ten kinds of cheesecake at that place of his. That and dog treats too. Going to expand the place; the place will be huge, he says. Well, that will be the day! He can't even fill up the tiny space he has." Then she smirked at Toby. "It's probably that woman. I'll bet he has set his sights on impressing her."

"What woman would that be?"

"Oh, you know the one. Is it Sadie? Saundra?" She paused in her confusion. "I remember! Saudade! Weirdest name I ever heard."

Toby frowned. "I don't believe she's on my route, but what an intriguing name. Who is this Saudade?"

"Well, now how would I know that? I just know the man is troubled. Although most of it, I suspect, he brings on himself. And when he's at his lowest, he will sometimes say her name. Like at the grocery counter when he's 'just a little short.' Or when I'm the only one in that little shop of his, eating a stale doughnut and choking down the weakest coffee in the entire world. He will throw his arms up and in a mournful voice, the man will call out, 'Saudade!' As if she could come running and clean up his mess."

Toby winked. "Or perhaps he wants to make things better for the sake of his beloved. Love can ignite a fire of ambition in an ordinary man."

"Ridiculous," scoffed Frances. "Bill Butterick most certainly does not have a beloved."

"What check was he expecting?" Toby checked his bag again.

Frances shook her head. "Well, as you say, pie in the sky. This was supposedly a check from some quiz show on TV. Bill is claiming he won thousands."

"You know, that one could be true." Toby raised an eyebrow. "Jeff Bezos was a fry cook in his younger days. Do not be quick to judge the quality of a man's intelligence by the work he does. Bill is a man of great misfortune, and he lacks a certain savoir faire, but he still could be a genius. Genius is found among men who fail as well as those who thrive."

"Yeah, yeah, yeah," said Frances. "You go on with your mail. If you talked a little less, perhaps more of our stuff would land in our boxes instead of who-knows-where."

Frances had a point. Toby loved to talk! But the thing about Toby was, he could be kind of quiet if you caught him off his rounds. It was almost as if he saved the good stuff—the dispensing of the wisdom and the great good cheer—for when he was on the job. That wasn't *always* true, of course. Sometimes the Toby you saw out in the world was the exact same Toby who handed you your mail. But I decided he felt free not to be so jolly when he was off the clock—which I supposed was fair. I figured men like Toby, who liked to think deep thoughts, needed time for quiet too.

The last time I was at the bank, for instance, he most decidedly did *not* seem glad to see me. Oh, he was polite enough, but in that brief instant before I joined him in the line, I had seen his face fall before he quickly rearranged his features into the familiar smile.

Once I saw him take the long route to his car to avoid crossing paths with me as I headed into the flea market to browse through the vintage books. And he *pointedly* avoided me not long after that. It was at the diner where I used to meet Andi every Wednesday. Embarrassed to be lunching with a pretty blonde who was half his age? Good for them, I'd say. It was not my business!

The dramatic part of me liked to think my postman had a secret life. Some people in this town surely did.

Now, he lifted his hand in a wave. "See you tomorrow, Frances. I will look forward then to another pleasant talk."

She squinted over to her left, then an angry look moved across her face. "There he is again!" she growled.

"Who?"

"That awful cop with all his questions. If he would write my answers down, he wouldn't have to keep after me like this. And perhaps he'd leave my boys alone as well."

I turned to see Rick in his official car coming down the street. Scott must have let him know to take a harder look at Frances and her sons.

"What a nuisance." Frances shook her head.

"Well, now, there *has* been a horrendous murder, and you are the closest neighbor," Toby tried to reason with her.

"But even *before* Hannah died, that Rick Trimble was here all the time. Parked in front of Hannah's house, sometimes late at night. Now I ask you, Toby, is that a fitting place for a cop to park and stay all night? How likely was a crime to suddenly break out on a street like this, filled mainly with us old folks?"

Toby thought a minute. "Very strange," he said.

Very strange indeed. And also suspicious.

"Good morning!" Rick stepped out of the car, nodding at my neighbor and the mailman.

"Not so good anymore." Frances stared him down.

"I just had a few questions." Rick put his hands on his hips.

But I didn't hear the rest. I was staring at his car.

Genius that he was, he had left the car door open—which gave me an idea.

I didn't need to follow Rick.

Instead, I jumped right in the front seat. I was going for a ride.

CHAPTER SIX

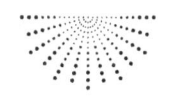

*R*ick arranged his features into a stern, official look as he took off way too fast down the main road in town. No way would his fellow drivers ever guess he was listening to atrocious music about walking in the rain and "love as fresh as spring." I rolled my eyes and wondered if I could have some cabernet to go with all the cheese.

For the first thirty minutes, give or take, he did nothing whatsoever to protect the people he was sworn to serve. Instead, he could have run a few down since he didn't slow for pedestrians at all. He seemed to take for granted that all of them would leap back when they saw him coming—in deference, of course, to his official status and his need for speed.

Then he stopped at the park, and we watched at a

distance while some guys, who appeared to be retirees, shot baskets for a while. Then suddenly, Rick sat up straight, alert. And for no reason I could see, he gunned the engine and let the siren screech. *Whoa.* I grabbed the dashboard for support after almost being thrown onto the floor. At least I couldn't die! *Been there, done that.*

I was a little pumped as I kept my hands braced on the dashboard and watched the scenery fly by. As crazy as it sounds, I always kind of wanted to ride along with a cop. Well maybe not *this* cop—but whatever. In second grade, when three-fourths of the class chose "veterinarian" for their career-day presentations, I was the only kid who came in dressed up like a cop. Well, now I kind of *was* one—on a major case. It was just too bad I was the victim too.

Rick picked up some speed as he flew down Main Street, slowing but not stopping for a series of red lights.

Where exactly was he going? He had not received a call. But now we must've been getting closer to wherever we were going; he was starting to slow down. And then we arrived at the Burger Barn, where he whipped in quickly to the parking lot, almost crashing into some startled lady's Cadillac.

I glanced around for hints about what might be going on. Hopefully the Burger Barn wasn't getting robbed; the owner was a nice guy who came in quite a bit for our half-price Tuesday nights. Perhaps it was a fight, but everything looked calm with the parking lot half empty.

Suddenly, Rick killed the siren and whipped around the side of the parking lot, pulling up to the drive-through window.

"Are you for real?" I screamed.

I guess he thought, *Why bother with red lights when you have a siren and a craving for a burger?*

This was their best guy to put on Colby Pointe's first murder case in years? Of course, I could only hope the man was just inept and not some kind of crook, as I was starting to suspect.

He turned down the bad music. "I will have the Barnyard Special with a Coke and extra fry," he announced into the speaker.

With no cars in front of us, he quickly had his bag of food, and we were back on the road. Driving at a somewhat normal speed now, he chewed in time to the music, nodding his head to the beat. After ten or fifteen minutes, we arrived at Silver's Gym, which was owned by Ed Lincoln, Frances's oldest son. Now we were getting somewhere. Perhaps Rick could indeed squeeze some investigating into his routine.

He pulled right up to the entrance and slammed the

door as he got out, as if to announce his presence. Then we headed into the lobby, where a middle-aged woman was signing in at the front desk. About a dozen people were scattered about the large space, running on treadmills, lifting weights, and working out in a variety of ways. Most of them had on headphones and seemed lost in their own worlds.

When the woman in front of us had signed in, Rick pulled out his badge. "Rick Trimble, Colby Pointe PD." He spoke in a booming voice that seemed at odds with his slight frame. "I'm here to speak to Ed."

"If you will wait right here, sir," said the young receptionist, "I will get him now." A tiny bit of fear seeped through the professional polish of her tone.

In a flash, Ed appeared. With dark, swarthy features, he was on the short side but had the physique of a pro wrestler. He must make good use of those weights lying around "the office," I decided. He stuck his hand out to Rick, but there was not a hint of friendliness in the man's expression. "What can I do for you today?"

"We're doing follow-up on the Hannah Jenkins murder," Rick explained. "We've spoken to the neighbors about anything suspicious they might have noticed at her house—strangers on the street, odd noises, such as that. I understand you are frequently next door to look in on your mother, and I just had some questions." Rick pulled a notebook from his pocket.

The blonde receptionist stared at her computer screen, trying to appear not to be listening in.

Ed sighed, his hands on his hips. "I have received your messages, your *many* messages, and I don't have a clue about who might have killed that girl. If I could help, I would. But as you can see, this is a place of business, and I do have work to do." There was a challenge in his voice.

"Just a few simple questions and you can get on with your day," Rick reassured him. "I am sure you will agree it's a matter of some urgency that a vicious killer be taken off the streets of Colby Pointe."

"Well, I was just about to lift some weights." Ed shrugged. "How about you can ask your questions while I do my routine?" He stood up a little straighter as if to show off his muscles. "Got to work on the pecs."

"Well, I suppose that's fine. I myself have been known to lift some weights," said Rick, who looked like he might struggle with a sack of potatoes.

We headed to a far corner of the gym, where Ed lifted a dumbbell over each shoulder as they talked. He explained he was at his mother's once or twice a week. Sometimes it was three times if Frances, on a whim, got the urge to bake.

"How well did you know Hannah?" Rick's pen was poised over his notebook.

"I didn't know her really except to wave sometimes if I saw her in the yard. Every now and then I might see her at the movies. Hey, did you see *Titanic*? That was quite a show."

We had shown the film during Oscar week along with several others that had won Best Picture through the years.

Rick shook his head and chuckled. "Makes a man think twice about going on some fancy cruise."

"Oh, yeah, I thought the same." Ed lifted the dumbbells up then down. "But then I told myself it was just a movie. It's not like the ship was real."

"Um, Ed." Rick scratched behind his ear. "That was based on something true. The Titanic really sank. All those people really died. It was kind of a big deal."

Ed paused with the dumbbells halfway up. "Well, now, you don't say." He resumed his lifting. "I hate to hear that, Rick. What an awful thing."

Rick coughed. "Well, back to the Hannah thing. Anyone suspicious you saw on the street?"

"Are you kidding me?" Ed scowled. "The place is crawling with them!" He paused his exercising to look Rick in the eye. "My mom is elderly, and you know what that means. People see an old lady in her yard, and they see 'easy target.' Why, there were two of them just the other day who showed up out of nowhere and promised her some pine straw in exchange for a check. And of course they stole her money." A dark look crossed his face as he put the dumbbells down and picked up some that looked even heavier. "If I could get my hands on those guys..."

I found myself inching away from Ed even though he couldn't see me. You wouldn't want to run into this guy at night if he thought you'd hurt his mother. Let's say, for example, in a lonely parking lot at the Yellow House. Would he have believed Frances if she told him I had stolen from her? Or did he know her mind was slipping? He seemed to spend a lot of time with Frances, but then again, he seemed to exercise his muscles more than he did his brain.

I hopped on a nearby treadmill to try to rid myself of some nervous energy.

Both men stared at the machine.

"Did that thing just switch on by itself?" asked Rick. "I'd get that fixed if I were you." Then he cleared his throat. "Could you describe these guys who came around about the pine straw?"

"I never saw the guys! But it doesn't matter. They were just the latest in a whole parade of thugs trying to steal from an old woman. The week before, she gave someone else a check when they came to the door selling *light bulbs* of all things. Can you believe the things that people get away with? My mother paid a fortune, and the things wouldn't even work." He gripped his hand tightly around the next weight he picked up. Then he lifted it above his head. "Those people better hope they don't come face to face with me, or it might be face to *fist*."

Or hands to throat perhaps? I ran a little faster.

Next, Rick asked about Ed's brother. "We have been unsuccessful making contact. Do you know when and where I might locate Les just to have a word?"

"Oh, I can't keep up with Les. He's always out of town on business. I think he might be in Dallas. Or is this week San Francisco?"

"Well, that's too bad." Rick shrugged and left his card on a stack of mats near Ed. "Let me know if you hear."

Then he said goodbye, and we were off, ending up in Rick's office at the station—which was the worst place for me to be. I could *not* run into Scott. I was getting ready to slip out when something caught my eye on Rick's desk, where he was busy playing Candy Crush on his big-screen computer. Beside him was a heavy notebook with cursive words in blue ink crowding the first page. The writing was illegible almost, but the thing that caught my eye was my own name. These must be notes about my case, I thought. I bent down to look more closely.

On the coffee-stained notebook paper were a zillion facts on me. And the thing about it was, the paper had a date written on the top: *three days before I died.*

Rick had recorded details of the schedule I had kept in life: What time my lights normally went out at night and when they came on the next morning. What days of the week I worked and my normal hours. The restaurants and other places that I liked to go and when. Rick, in fact, had taken detailed notes about when I came and went, including times and dates I went to the bank, the post office, and to get trims at the salon. He'd written down information that could only be known by peeking through my window: what I watched on television, who I called and when, and where I kept my purse and keys.

A chill ran through me as I read.

I ducked when I heard a rapping on the door and the sound of heavy footsteps as someone walked in the door.

Rick quickly tapped some buttons, and an "Incident Report" replaced his game on the screen.

"How's it going, Chief?" he asked.

Thank goodness that it wasn't Scott. I got up from my crouch.

Chief Matt Maloney was a tall man with an easy-going smile—someone else that I would miss. I felt the sense of loss that always came when I ran into a friend who would simply look right through me if I tried to say hello.

If I were alive, Matt might be handing me a piece of wrapped candy from his pocket, as if I were a kid. Scott said he kept the candy to give out to kids who were undergoing trauma of some kind.

"How's it going, Trimble?" asked the chief. "Any progress on the big case? Anything you need from me?"

Rick leaned back in his chair. "I've been going hard at it today. Had quite a lengthy chat with Ed Lincoln at the gym, and I pushed him hard on where we might find Les. I got an alibi on Ed, and his story did check out. Turns out he was at a sports bar the night that Hannah died. I went straight there to confirm it once I finished at the gym."

I couldn't stand to hear any more of the braggart's lies. I was out of there. But first there was a little something that I had to do, a bit of information to communicate to Matt. On my way out the door, I knocked the notebook to the floor.

Rick scrambled to grab it, but the chief was closer and he beat Rick to pick it up.

"How did that even happen?" Matt looked around, confused. "It was like this notebook just decided to take off and fly right off your desk." Then he glanced down at the paper in his hand, and a wrinkle appeared on his brow. "Trimble, what is this?"

"Well, boss, I...well, I..." As Rick stumbled to explain, I heard someone call out in the hall. "Hey! How's it going, Scott?"

Whoops. That voice had sounded close. It was time to disappear, and disappear I did—underneath Rick's desk.

In a case of awful timing, someone knocked just as the drama had begun to escalate between Rick and Matt.

"Chief! We need you stat," said an officer whose voice was coming from the doorway.

"On my way," said Matt.

Well, shoot. I debated staying under there to see if he came back. But I knew from Scott how many directions those guys got pulled in every day. It could be a while before Matt returned, and it was a mess down there—kind of sickening, really. I could hear Scott right outside, so I would have to stay underneath the desk if I were to stick around.

No, thanks. I looked around me in disgust at the million candy wrappers and other bits of trash. Did the guy not understand how to use the trash can that was *right beside his desk?* Plus, there were dust bunnies everywhere. It was a little crowded, too, with stacks of brown-paper packages pushing into my side. A pile of letters had been placed neatly on the top.

Hmm. I looked down to inspect the stash.

"Anything that's out of place—that could be a clue," Scott had told me once as we watched some detective thriller at the Yellow House. It made absolutely no sense for Rick to stuff the mail underneath the desk, where it would be bumping constantly against his feet. There was room to put the boxes in any of the four corners of the office or against the long wall to the left. It almost seemed like Rick had a reason to keep the boxes hidden. I glanced at the top one, addressed to some woman in Montana with the return address of a woman here in town. The whole thing was just odd.

But best to think about it out in the fresh air, which was why I disappeared from the police station altogether.

It was a simple matter to just close my eyes and reappear out on the sidewalk, about a block away and safe from the eyes of Scott. As much as possible, I tried to come and go like a living person would, holding on to any bit of "normal" that I could. But I did love the thought of being anywhere I wanted—and of disappearing quickly when the need arose.

The day had turned cooler as I made my way back home, still stunned by the extent of how closely Rick had been watching me in the days before I died. I tried to calm my mind by singing a few bars of "Shake it Off," but it was no use. Celeste had told me that I would at some point feel an "easing" from this world, a sense of things not mattering as much as they used to. Well, I was not there yet; I was furious and struggling to even breathe in a normal fashion.

Then as I neared my house, I saw a flash of yellow on my porch, and I smiled—although I was confused. What was Nacho doing there? I'd never seen her anywhere except at the Yellow House. She had never been a cat to roam around or get any exercise at all. If she wasn't snacking, she was curled up for a nap. But now the big cat looked alert as I walked up the drive, and then she trotted toward me.

I stared at her in shock. "Nacho! Can you *see* me?"

Her answer was an affirmative meow.

I sank down on the steps, and she crawled into my lap, which she never did, even with the living. We used to joke that she liked our treats much more than she liked us. Alison, my boss, figured that the cat just wasn't used to people. But she'd become a familiar presence at the Yellow House. Whenever one of us would sneak her a treat, someone would have to say it: *That is "na cho" cat.*

But she *was* our cat. Very fully ours. An orangish-yellow cat for the Yellow House.

Now, she pushed her head into my chest, snuggled in, and purred. Tears pricked at my eyes as I rubbed her fur. For the first time it fully hit me how isolated I had been. Having only Scott to talk to had been bad enough, but now I'd lost him as well.

As if she could read my thoughts, Nacho lifted a paw and held it gently against my cheek. With her soft warmth against me, I realized my breathing had gone back to normal, and I suddenly felt calm. The universe must have noticed I was struggling and sent me a friend.

After a while, she moved into a patch of sun to nap. Watching her, I yawned and pulled my cell phone from my pocket, surprised to see I had no messages or texts. Then I remembered why. Old habits, they die hard.

I scrolled through social media, which was, frankly, sad. Three of my best friends had spent the day at the Salty Daze Beach Fest, where I always bought a sea-glass ring from a gray-haired man who recognized me every year and told me a bad joke. It had become our thing. Over the years, I had collected rings in six different colors. I liked to line them up on my bedroom window, where they caught the morning light.

Then I looked at the last picture. My friends were holding up their hands to show a rainbow of green and blue and purple on their fingers, sparkling in the sun. "For Hannah," said the caption.

Nacho had woken up and was sniffing at the bushes along the front of the house. Then she began to bat feverishly at something deep within the greenery. For such a laid-back cat, Nacho seemed excited, so I got up to look.

At first it seemed to be just a wad of tissue that was just out of her reach, but then I caught a glint of silver winking out at me.

"Nacho, what did you find?" I pulled out the little package to discover a fancy silver spoon. It was still halfway wrapped in the tissue. *Hmm.* I carefully unwrapped it, and I gasped when I got a closer look. I had gone along on enough antiquing trips with Maria Claire to recognize real silver. And that looked like a real ruby in the center of the handle—a ruby that was very large. Still tucked in the tissue was a little card with the name of a store. Antiquities and Wonders was a place where I sometimes liked to browse but could never buy. It catered to the rich-retiree set who could afford to follow the dictates of their whims, no matter how absurd the prices.

I sat back on the steps to examine it some more, wishing I could talk about this weird clue with Scott. Had Rick dropped it, or had Bill?

Nacho had settled at my feet and gone back to her

nap. Given her dislike of moving, that productive little dig must have tired her out.

"Well, I see you have a friend." Suddenly, Celeste was seated on the step beside me. Today she had her curls piled high up on her head.

By now, I was not surprised at the way she came and went.

"Celeste, the cat can see me!" I gently ran my finger along Nacho's back, still in awe.

"Yeah, sometimes that can happen." She twisted the sparkly bracelet on her wrist. "Animals are smart, and some of them can see things that people can't."

I remembered the way Cleopatra had seemed to sense that I was there. Oh, how much I wished she could see me too. Then we could maybe play a round of "keep away" out in Andi's yard; Cleopatra loved that game.

"Oh!" I paused dramatically. "I have some news for you while we are on the subject of who can and cannot see those of us who are dead."

She turned to me, alert.

"I am not the only one who has hung out with the living at the Yellow House," I told her breathlessly. "Other ghosts—or whatever we are called—have been talking to live people. They've been doing it for years!"

She gasped. "What do you mean?"

I told her what I'd learned about the dead glitterati

who had hung out in the lobby. "And the stories that I heard, those are just examples; there are other stories too." I paused to take a breath. "It's like the Yellow House is a whole big party—for the living *and* the dead."

Then I thought of something: why had *I* never seen a ghost? I'd spent eight hours a day or more at the Yellow House while I was alive!

But then again, perhaps I had *felt* a ghost.

A memory came back. One night the year before, a feeling of intensity and dread had settled over me as I sat alone in Theatre 3C. I was stuffing chocolate into my mouth as Sylvia Plath's life story unfolded on the screen. Like the good English major that I was, I had known going in how *that* was going to end. But still. It was a different kind of sadness than I had ever felt before. Had *she* been beside me for a moment so that I could feel her pain? For just a tiny while, it had felt that real.

I turned to Celeste, who stared at me, wide-eyed. Then—just like that—she was gone.

I stared at the empty space, which kind of glittered in her absence.

Then she reappeared. "Sorry about that!" She nervously touched her hair. "It's just that this is a shock. The bosses, I am almost sure, have *no idea* this is going on. And, Hannah, this is huge. This is unprecedented! And a little terrifying." She reached out to touch my hand. "They were so alarmed when they thought it was only you, and now... Well, I really need to get back and sound the alarm."

"But wait!" I held tightly to her hand, as if that could really stop her from disappearing. "Before you go, Celeste, don't you think this means that I can talk to Scott?" *Please tell me that I can.* My voice turned almost pleading. "Because now we know: ghosts and living people have been mingling for years, and the world is *still okay!* So it shouldn't hurt if *one more ghost* spent a little time with someone that she loves."

"Well, that *does* make sense." But Celeste looked confused. "Oh, Hannah, I don't know. Any change in rules cannot come from me. That must be decided on a *much* higher level." She looked in my eyes. "Hannah, hold that thought."

Before I could beg her to hurry back with news, Celeste was gone.

CHAPTER SEVEN

I went inside and made myself a chicken salad sandwich. Nacho came in too, and I found some tuna for her. That seemed to make it official: I was her new best friend. Her nose disappeared into the bowl of tuna before I could even set it down. Then once the food was gone, she licked the dish and settled down for still another nap.

While I ate my sandwich, I picked up my phone and pulled up the website for Antiquities and Wonders. I found the spoon right away in a section at the top called "Some of Our Favorite Things." I clicked on the picture and just about choked on my bite of sandwich. I could not believe my eyes. More than *four hundred dollars* for a single spoon! Who in the world would pay that and, more importantly, who would have left it in my yard? I knew that Bill and Rick and Frances all had been there and would have had the chance to drop it, but none of them were wealthy. I imagined they would buy any spoons they needed at Values Galore, where I liked to shop. In fact, I would love to hear one of the sales staff recommend to Frances that she buy a spoon for four-hundred-plus. Her reaction would be priceless!

Once my meal was finished, I prepared my house for a cat. I found a litter box and toys left over from the time I watched a cat for one of the ticket sellers at the Yellow House. Then I glanced down at Nacho, curled up in an orange ball, and decided that a nap seemed like a nice idea. So I stretched out on the couch with my favorite purple blanket.

Forty minutes later, I woke up with a sweet tooth and decided I would head to Doughnut Delights and More, where hopefully the "more" would be a clue about Bill's trip to the park. I scratched behind Nacho's ears, careful not to wake her. "Be back a little later," I whispered to the cat, "and maybe I'll bring treats."

I arrived at Bill's to find the tables empty except for one that was occupied by an older woman with a half-finished doughnut and a mug of coffee. It was

Viola Tripp, which meant Bill had almost surely comped the food. The merchants in the center suspected she was homeless, and we all did what we could to help. But Bill seemed to be the only one with time to listen to her stories, most of which began, "When I was a girl back in Portugal…" She pushed her stringy hair out of her eyes before she took a sip of coffee.

Up toward the ceiling to my left, a TV was playing softly while Bill wiped the tables, humming to himself. The counter was lined with Star Wars figures, and photographs were taped onto the wall behind the register. In one of the photos, two young boys were laughing as they tried to push each other into a swimming pool. In another, several toddlers were piled into a woman's lap.

Viola focused the photos as she slowly chewed her doughnut. "Nice family you have, Bill. I didn't know that you had kids."

"Oh, no. No kids for me." Bill paused in his work. "Would you believe I found these pictures in a rummage sale? Stacks and stacks of pictures!" A shadow crossed his face as he glanced at the photos. "Now, how sad is that? Someone was selling pictures of their *family*, selling them to strangers, ten pictures for a dime! Is that what a family's worth?"

Viola frowned. "In my day in Portugal, things were *very* different. People had respect."

Bill stared at the photos. "They look like nice kids, right? These all look like nice people. And I thought they looked alone there in the box, and I'm alone as well. So I just brought them here! To brighten up the place." He folded up his rag, placed it behind the counter, and poured a cup of coffee.

Both of them fell quiet, and the only voices came from the TV.

"In *The Canterbury Tales*," asked a man on the screen, "where did the pilgrims gather?"

The contestants stared blankly at the white-toothed host.

"Tabard Inn," said Bill, picking up his mug.

"Who discovered the Rosetta Stone?"

"The *what* stone?" asked Viola.

"The Rosetta Stone," said Bill. "And it was discovered by Pierre François Bouchard."

I wondered if maybe Bill truly had a reason to expect that prize check in the mail.

While he stared at the TV, I snuck a doughnut from the case and left a bill on the counter.

Viola, in the meantime, stuffed the last bit of her doughnut into her mouth. "You could have made a fine life, Bill, with that brain of yours," she said.

"Well, you either get the breaks or not. And I like to think I provide my customers with a little treat in the middle of the day. That will have to be enough."

"I understand." She picked up her mug. "I wanted lots of things as well."

"I was all about the science." Bill took a sip of his drink. "I was gonna be the man who does the weather on TV. I had it all planned out, and then everything went wrong."

She nodded. "Saudade!"

She knew about this Saudade?

In the thirty or so minutes I was in the shop, the only visitors were an older couple who bought one doughnut apiece, and a young girl who asked to use the restroom. When he wasn't calling out right answers, Bill made two brief calls, both of them boring stuff with no clues at all about why I'd had to die—or why Bill had buried a strange box in the middle of the night.

With her doughnut finished, Viola began to fold a napkin into the shape of a bird. When Bill was finished with his calls, she looked up from her art. "Sounds like you have made some nice plans for the week," his eavesdropping guest observed.

"Well, I help out when I can." Bill took a sip of coffee. "Lot of needs in Colby Pointe, and a man like me has time to spare." He shrugged. "So I take Dee Johnson out for a fish dinner every Tuesday. She cannot see to drive, and a widow in poor health needs to get out now and then."

"Well, that is nice," Viola said.

"And Kate Dayton comes along with us most days. Since her husband died last year, she likes a night out as well." He paused. "My mother raised me to be a gentleman, you know, so I take care of the ladies." He let out a sigh. "Although in some cases, I have failed. And failed to be a gentleman as well."

What did he even mean? Was that related to the box?

"And I've seen you in the park with all the dogs, lots and lots of dogs." Viola smoothed a folded edge on one wing of her bird.

"Yes, that fills up my Wednesdays, and the shelter's glad to have me. The dogs need the exercise, the sunshine, and I guess I do as well." Bill chuckled as he touched his belly, which ballooned over his belt.

"I hear you have a house full."

"I am the proud papa of four dogs and one cat," Bill said with a smile. "I guess that's one advantage of the single life. No wife at home to put a limit on the pets."

Interesting, I thought. This man takes widows out on Tuesdays, walks shelter dogs on Wednesdays, and on a recent Thursday, he had…maybe *murdered* me? Something didn't fit.

STRANGLED AT THE CINEMA

The man was up to *something*, sneaking into my yard in the middle of the night. Plus, he had been absolutely livid on that day he accused me of "stealing" doughnut sales. He was normally mild-mannered, almost to a fault. Had he simply snapped?

Hopefully, Celeste would be back soon to tell me I could talk to Scott. With Scott's detective skills and my ability to go anywhere and see anything, we could wrap this case up quickly. In the meantime, though, I was on my own.

Perhaps I could do a little wandering, with my ears wide open, through Antiquities and Wonders. Someone at the store might have gotten word that the little spoon, still in its tissue, had been lost. With the price the customer had paid, that would have been quite the story, and Colby Pointe was full of talkers.

As I took my last bite of doughnut and headed out the door, I felt a surge of hope. If I could somehow figure out who was connected to that spoon, that would tell me who had been deep in my front-yard bushes not long before I died. The tissue had shown no signs of being weathered; it could not have been there long.

On my way to Antiquities, I passed the Yellow House, where four men in suits were filing out the door. There was something odd about them—and it wasn't just that hardly anybody went to see a movie in a suit and tie. There was a paleness to their features despite the temperatures that had left almost everybody either burned or tan that week.

When the shortest one winked at me as I passed, I suddenly understood: they had come from *there*. Celeste's bosses, it appeared, hadn't wasted any time in sending down a crew to investigate what was going on at the Yellow House.

I wondered what they'd found as I walked another block to Antiquities and Wonders. The shop, when I arrived, looked grand and inviting. On either side of the double doors were pots of tall white flowers with lush and vibrant greenery. Soft music seemed to welcome me as I stepped inside. The carpet felt like a pillow for my feet, and two candles on the counter sent a faint lavender aroma wafting through the room.

No one was inside, however, to enjoy these luxuries except for me and the two women behind the counter in the front.

As I browsed in the jewelry section, it did not take long for the subject of the spoon to come up. The women must have been talking about the missing treasure before I arrived.

"Well it is a shame," said the younger one, a tall blonde, who was straightening a display of fancy pens. "But everyone should know not to send a thing like that in *the US mail*." Her name tag identified her as "Zoe."

The shorter, gray-haired woman shook her head. "She could have simply driven the *two blocks* to hand the present to her daughter. But no one, I suppose, has time for that today. It's all gift certificates and sticking items in the mail because we're all too busy. And don't even get me started on how we can't trust the mail."

I peeked at her name tag. The older woman's name was "Kay."

The younger woman pulled a cloth from behind the counter to polish a gold pen studded with green jewels. "Not in Colby Pointe, we can't." She looked around and lowered her voice, despite the fact there were no customers around. I guessed no one had a spare four hundred dollars to spend on a spoon!

"My cousin works with the police as a secretary," Zoe continued, "and she tells me there have been some issues regarding stolen mail."

Frances had been right!

"She was telling me they'd found a whole bag of abandoned mail behind an old shed near the lake," Zoe explained. "Someone had apparently gone through it to look for things that might have value—like a House of Healey spoon." She rolled her eyes.

"So many of our customers are getting on in years,"

said Kay with a sigh. "I think it would behoove us to remind them of some basic safety rules—like being very careful what they put in the mail. If it was my mother in the store, I would hope someone would do the same."

"They think the thief has also taken things out of people's boxes." Zoe had finished with her pens and sat down on a stool. "Or I guess it could be a whole *gang* of thieves. The cops went through the items in the bag, checked for fingerprints, and returned all of the stuff to the postal service."

But not *all* of it perhaps. Had Rick decided to go through the stolen stuff and keep some things for himself, stashed beneath his desk? Were there checks in those envelopes stacked on the packages? And had he dropped one very pricey item in my bushes when he came to spy on me?

I *had* to talk to Scott!

Trying to distract myself from dark thoughts, I wandered through the aisles. I picked up a crystal vase.

Then I was startled by a voice.

"Absolutely gorgeous!" Celeste was twirling next to me. A blue and silver shawl from Antiquities was wrapped around her shoulders. Then she touched the fabric, and her eyes went soft. "I remember silk." Her voice was an almost whisper.

Something in her expression made me wonder for the first time who my Guide had been.

"Who were you?" I asked her softly. "You know, before you died?"

"Oh, I wasn't anyone who could afford to dress like this." She ran her fingers down the shawl. "But every now and then, I'd splurge on something pretty, and I'd go out and dance." She paused to listen to the music playing in the shop. "You know, it mostly goes away, the longing for the earth, but there still are times…"

I grabbed her hand and squeezed. "I know."

"Oh, but you can't imagine how it is up there!" Celeste's eyes were shining. She picked up a tiny dish. "It's just that sometimes I miss dancing and the smell of men's cologne and…well, do you ever have a moment when you can't stop laughing no matter how you try? Sometimes I miss that. They say it's because I'm new."

Zoe walked past with a box and shivered. "Do you feel a draft?" she called to Kay.

Celeste winked at me, tying the shawl artfully around her shoulders. "I have come with news." She smiled. "News you're gonna like!" she teased.

"I can talk to Scott?" I asked her breathlessly.

She picked up a jeweled comb and arranged it in my hair. "*You* have to dress up, girl. You get to see your man!"

I gave her a hug then did a little dance. "Celeste! What did they say?"

"Well, first of all, they were absolutely shocked. They could not believe it! So they sent down a crew."

"I saw them coming out of the Yellow House. Your people, they work fast."

"Not really all that fast for an emergency," she said. "Time there and time here—it moves in different ways. Plus, they saw this as a crisis. Just you by yourself were an emergency, and this just upped the stakes. But thank goodness, all is well." She breathed a sigh of relief. "In fact, they were very pleased."

I stared at Celeste. "First there was the fuss about 'no interaction,' and now suddenly they're *pleased?*"

"Oh, yes, it's quite amazing—although a big surprise. There's apparently a gateway that runs between our world and yours. We had no idea! It runs just to the left of the projection room at the Yellow House."

"Only one of these in the entire world, and it's here in Colby Pointe?" It had always felt to me like a special place, but this was surreal.

"We *think* there's only one. At first, none of my bosses could believe it was even possible—but then there it was. Cosmic Security confirmed it."

"But I still don't get it. If they were so freaked out

that I could talk to Scott, why are they so happy that these other ghosts have been doing the same thing?"

"Because an energy of protection has been found to emanate from around the gate. If a spirit tries to come in with the intent to harm, the passageway will close until the spirit is no longer close." She paused. "Mostly, the 'visitors' seem to make their way to the gate through the medium of films. Sometimes they're performers, or someone has made a movie about something they lived through." She touched my hand. "So Hannah, it's all good." She let out a sigh. "I was kind of feeling pressure to...well, not to let the world *explode.* Since all of this seemed to start with someone in my care. Talk about a bad day at work."

"But why me?" I asked, still confused. "I'm not in the movies! Why am I still here?"

"I guess as a...reward? The Yellow House, it turns out, is a very special place. And in your short time in your new role, you were important to the process. You brought in the stories of the dead—to teach the lessons that the dead could no longer tell."

"Well, thanks." I could feel my face turn red.

"And you could not have passed through unless the work you had left to do was pure—and would not interfere with important parts of the master plan." She paused. "We have always known that people in the arts are special—those who work in films and music and the like. They are the ones most likely to sense the other worlds at the edges of their own."

"Those in the arts—and pets."

"Yes, the animals as well." She paused. "So go solve your murder, Hannah." She gave me a wink. "And enjoy your time with Scott."

"But can't *you* tell me now, in light of everything we know? Why did I have to die—and who killed me, Celeste?" After all my agonizing, I was almost scared to hear what she might have to say.

"You must find the answers for yourself," she told me gently, "but you *will* find them, Hannah. That is why you're here." Celeste watched me sadly. "Hannah, see you soon."

And then she was gone.

As I headed to the station to see Scott, it was all I could do not to run. As I passed the doughnut shop, Bill was stepping out for air at the very moment Rick was strutting past his door. Bill gave him a glare.

Hmm. Had Rick done his job for once and asked Bill some probing questions about the night I died? Or had Bill seen some things? Did he know Rick was a snake?

Andi strolled by next with Cleopatra. This little square of sidewalk was a busy place! Cleopatra growled at Rick, and Andi pulled nervously on her leash. "What's the matter, girl?" she asked in a gentle voice. "Come on, you're okay!"

The pug whined a bit and sniffed the air when she got to the spot where I was standing.

I miss you too, I thought.

"What's wrong, Cleopatra?" Andi asked the dog, confused. "I've never seen you growl, and now you look so sad."

Then Cleopatra began barking fiercely when Toby came around the corner with some mail for Bill.

He smiled and held his hands up. "Hey, Cleopatra, you remember me! I bring you mail and treats!"

Andi smiled apologetically at him. "She must be missing Hannah; she must be so confused about where Hannah went."

Bill knelt by his door. "Is that Miss Cleopatra that I see?" he asked in a warm tone.

At the sound of his voice, the pug yipped happily and jumped up on his legs.

He laughed and scratched behind her ears. "I would say you're glad to see me, but I imagine you're just hoping I can find a treat that has your name on it." Then he winked at Andi. "I've never had much luck with the ladies unless I hand out food."

He disappeared and came back with a dog treat, which Cleopatra happily scarfed down. She was acting strangely, but now she seemed to be okay. I sighed in relief as I continued on my way.

CHAPTER EIGHT

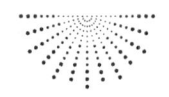

As I got closer to the station, I began to run. *Scott!* I could be with Scott.

I was halfway there when I remembered: *Silly me!* I could close my eyes, and I could be there *now*. I paused to picture his cramped office and his familiar frame behind his neatly ordered desk. I let the magic do its work and—just like that—I was there.

Luckily, he was there by himself working on reports. I watched him for a moment as he cocked his head in that way he had, trying to decide if the notes on his computer held a clue he might have somehow missed.

I teased him with one of his own "lessons" from our time in the Yellow House watching movies about cops. "It's the husband or the maid," I said. "It's the one you least suspect!"

He looked up. "Hannah!"

I had carefully rehearsed my explanation for disappearing in the park, but once his arms were around me, there was no need for talk. I knew him, and he knew me; he knew I would have stayed with him if I could—if the rules of this crazy new existence had not swept me away.

"You're here," he said in awe. He kissed me like a man who felt a kiss hello might also mean goodbye.

"We have some time," I reassured him, my fingers trailing down his face. "Until this thing is solved, they've told me I can stay. I've been here all along, but...well, it's complicated." I touched my forehead to his. "Scott, I have some things to tell you." But where to even start? "I think Rick might be the one who...well, he might be the one who hurt me in the parking lot that night."

"*Rick?* Hannah, there's no way!" Scott pulled back to stare at me.

"I've been watching him, you see." I took a breath and put my hand in Scott's. "And the thing about it is...that all along Rick was watching *me*." I explained about the notes I'd seen and how they proved Scott's fellow cop had been a creepazoid, peeking in my window at all hours of the day and night.

Scott's face went tight with fury. "What in the..." He

paused to calm himself. With his hands on his hips, he stared down at the worn carpet, breathing in and out. "Hannah, I am shocked. I cannot fathom why on earth Rick would...well, I can't even say the words." He took another calming breath. "The guy has always been an oddball, not the smartest, maybe. But *a stalker*, Hannah? How could I not have known?" He thought some more, still staring at the carpet, then he looked up at me. "You know, now I wonder if Matt is onto him. I saw those two earlier, and Matt looked absolutely livid, like he would have loved to punch a hole right through Rick's sorry face."

"Oh, Matt knows for sure. Because I told him —kind of."

"You talked to Matt?" He stared at me, wide-eyed.

"Well, no. Not exactly. They were meeting in Rick's office, and I made sure a certain notebook went flying off the desk—with some incriminating notes. I aimed it at Matt's foot."

Scott managed a small smile. "That's impressive, Hannah." Then he sank down in his desk chair, his head in his hands. "I feel like such a fool that I didn't even know the guy I worked with every day was that kind of creep."

I moved to his lap. "Matt didn't see it either. Nobody saw it, Scott." We sat awhile in silence.

"Has he seemed different lately?" I asked after a while. "Like guilty? Nervous maybe?"

"He's been out of sorts a while. There's a new position opening next year, as assistant to the chief, and Rick was gunning for it. But he's not the greatest cop. Matt has been mostly putting Rick on low-priority assignments. And I think he finally understood there was no chance of him advancing."

"And Matt assigned him to *my* case?" *Gee, Matt, thanks a lot.*

"Well, for obvious reasons, Hannah, it could not be me. And one of the detectives is Bill's cousin, so that wouldn't do with Bill on the list of suspects. Our top investigator is on leave right now, so it was down to Rick. But Matt himself was investigating—and I was going at it hard. You were not forgotten, Hannah."

"Oh, I understand; I get it." I wound my hand in his. I paused for a moment. "Was Rick, by any chance, assigned to also work on that thing with the mail?"

"No. I was just pulled in the other day to head that one up myself. But how in the world did you...?"

I stood up, full of energy—and news. I told him about the packages underneath Rick's desk.

Scott stared at me, amazed. "What is this guy's game? He was after you, and now he's messing with my case?

All of that stuff was returned to the postal-service people—or that's what I was told."

"And he also dropped a package in my bushes when he was spying on me. Or I guess Bill could have dropped it since he was also doing *something* in my yard. Although we can't link Bill, I guess, to this business with the mail."

Scott shook his head at the name. "That Bill from the doughnut shop—he's another odd one. I have questioned that guy—twice."

"So you *have* been on my case."

"Of course!" Scott stood and walked around his desk to perch on the edge. "How could I just sit around doing unimportant things and *not* investigate?" He took a breath. "As it turns out, Bill has an alibi for…the night it happened. But he's hiding something, Hannah. He looked just devastated when we talked about it. Not in a 'she-was-too-young-to-die' way. In an 'I-did-something-awful' way."

I leaned against the window. "Well, he did speak to me rather harshly. And right after that, I died. That could be enough right there to make a guy feel pretty bad."

"I got the idea, though, something more was on his mind." Scott joined me at the window. "I canvassed the areas again—both around your neighborhood and at the shopping center around the Yellow House. Which really let me know what a sorry job Rick was doing with the case." Scott's eyes clouded over. "Of course, why question anyone at all if it was him all along who put his grubby hands around your neck?" He paused for some calming breaths. "Or if he was protecting someone else he knew was involved."

"Protecting someone? Who?"

Scott seemed to change the subject, his mind a million places. "Hannah, when I left you last, we were just about to find out what Bill Butterick had buried in the park. Were you able to find out?"

"Well, actually, I was—but I don't know if this will help." I explained about the rubber duck, the mitten, the hand-carved Star Wars chess set, and the tiger ears. "It all seems *very* unconnected to what happened to me."

Scott cocked his head to study me. "Those are just about the most nonsensical clues I think I have ever heard."

"And it gets even weirder. I saw the *matching mitten* after that! Frances, of all people, had it on."

"Interesting," he said. "Bill could have dropped it in your yard when he was there that night."

"Did he confess to being there?" I asked anxiously. "Scott, what did he say?"

Scott ran a hand through his hair. "At first he denied

it, but when I brought up the watch, he admitted he was there. And the reason was just odd. The guy swore up and down he felt you were *in danger.*" Scott gave a little shrug. "That is what he said. That if he himself had daughters, he would want to know someone was looking out for them."

"But that makes no sense! Before I got grabbed by that monster—by Rick or whoever—no one in my neighborhood was worried about safety."

"Here is how I see it." Scott leaned against the wall. "With no excuse for being at your house after midnight, with a known grudge against you, I am thinking maybe Bill could have played a hand in this."

That made me really sad, which was kind of weird—since I was already *dead.* How much sadder, really, could things get than *that?* "But why would they want me dead, either him or Rick?" I moved to the desk and sank down in Scott's chair.

"I haven't found a motive that makes any sense." Scott shook his head and sighed. "And Bill's alibi checked out; he was at a neighbor's cookout. First to arrive and last to leave. That was attested to by the fire chief, the assistant principal of Colby Pointe Middle School, and the head librarian. So he is about as alibied as a guy could get."

"So he *didn't* do it?!"

"But he could still be involved. Some of the people in your neighborhood—and some who work near the theater as well—reported something strange. Several of them told me Bill seemed to *shadow* Rick while Rick was making rounds just before you died. They said if they saw Rick, Bill was right there too, kind of in the background."

"Odd." I thought about it. "Could Bill have recognized Rick as the monster that he was? Could he have been protecting me from Rick?"

"That's one theory that I have, but given his behavior at the park and the fact that he was angry with you right before you died, I have to think it's possible that the two of them were working as a team."

As a team to kill me. Why?

"It's just a theory, Hannah."

A chill ran through me then. "Scott, I'm worried about someone. I think that maybe Bill was mad at someone else as well. Because, you see, there was a note. A note inside the box."

"A note?" Scott perked up at that.

"It was three words, Scott: 'Goodbye, goodbye, goodbye.'" I paused to watch his face. "Kind of creepy, right?"

"As in…he would maybe hurt himself?" Scott folded his arms, alarmed.

"Well, I hadn't thought of it in those terms. Because a

woman's name was written on the box. And since I thought Bill might have killed me, 'Goodbye, goodbye, goodbye' did not sound good for her." I paused. "Of course, it could have been a *man's* name—'Saudade.' Or a *place*. Who knows?"

Scott looked thoughtful. "I can see why you're concerned."

"It would be nice to warn her—but we don't know who she is."

"I could do a search for anyone with that name who might live nearby. Or see if someone by that name has been listed as a missing person." He moved to his computer, and his hands flew across the keys. "Let me start that search, but my gut is saying that we concentrate on Rick. I'd like to take a look at those packages he's hidden in his office."

"Let me slip in there, see if the coast is clear."

In two minutes I was back and gave Scott a nod. Then we headed down the hall hand in hand.

CHAPTER NINE

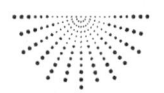

"How's it going, Scott?" asked Matt when we passed him in the hall.

I could tell the chief was preoccupied, and new wrinkles seemed to have formed around his eyes in the short time since I'd seen him. It made him look tired and old. "Stop by my office, please, when you get a minute. Something big has come up we need to discuss."

With a single nod, Scott said, "Give me a few minutes, sir, and I will be right in."

Scott put his arm around my waist as we continued to Rick's office. "That sounded ominous," he whispered as he quietly shut the door behind us. "Or was that my imagination?"

We moved behind Rick's desk, kneeling to check out the likely stolen loot.

Scott grabbed a stack of envelopes and quickly rifled through it. "Here's PTM Insurance; here's the IRS. All of these are places that routinely use the mail to send or receive big checks." He sighed. "And I imagine you can guess what Rick had planned to do with these."

"Well, I hate to tell you, but the stack looks smaller than before. His bank account might already be a lot fatter than before."

Scott shook his head. "What a screw-up this guy is."

The packages, for the most part, bore out Scott's theory too. I recognized the names of some expensive brands in the return addresses. There was Kate Spade; there was Apple. A few contained no brand names, but perhaps their heaviness—or words like "fragile" written across the front—had seemed promising to Rick.

"So what happens now?" I asked.

"I'll alert Matt to the problem. Then they'll want to question Rick and check his home for more. Might as well give Matt the news." He stood and held out his hand to help me up. Then we made the short walk down the hall.

Scott rapped politely on Matt's door, which was halfway open.

"Come on in and take a seat," said Matt.

Scott looked at the single chair, which I understood he wanted me to take—gentleman and all of that. "If it's just the same with you, sir, I would prefer to stand," he said. "Been sitting down all day. Lots and lots of desk work."

"Whatever works for you." Matt sighed and leaned back in his chair. "Listen, Scott, there have been some...irregularities that concern the transfer of the stolen mail to the postal service. Some of the mail on the master list was missing when the items were received—some of the more pricey items." A dark look crossed his face. "I don't need to tell you that does not make us look good. Sloppy in our work at best. Or in the worst case, dishonest." He rubbed at his forehead. "I put you on this case as it escalated because it needed brand new eyes—and because this one needs to be put to rest. This business of people not receiving mail has gotten this town up in arms. We must find this missing mail with no time to waste. Not that you're to blame," he hastened to add, "since you're brand new to the case."

"I am on it!" Scott said. "In fact, I can point you now to the missing mail, which I have located just this morning."

"Oh, thank goodness. That was fast! Somehow I had the feeling if I put you on the case, nothing would get past you."

"I'm afraid I've found the missing items—a lot of

them at least—underneath Rick's desk. It appears he tried to hide them."

Matt leaned forward and buried his face in his hands. "Please don't tell me that." Then he looked up at Scott. "I'm afraid Rick Trimble is not the man I thought. It has just come to my attention that he may have been involved in other things that were unknown to us. Which is why, as of this afternoon, I have put him on leave." Matt sighed. "Confidentially, I will tell you we have begun a review of Rick's activities with an eye to probable dismissal. And criminal charges, I'm afraid. And that was *before* we knew about this business with the mail." He studied Scott. "Any news on your end involving Hannah's case?"

"I'm now looking into several theories: that it might have a team, perhaps a slimeball stalker." Scott's look had turned hard.

Again, Matt looked surprised. "So you knew about the stalking. I am *doubly* impressed. I can confirm for you that she was being stalked, which is another matter I brought you in here to discuss." He paused. "This will be hard to hear, but we have evidence that *Rick* was the man who had been watching Hannah."

Scott stared at the chief, pretending to be shocked.

Matt explained about the detailed notes that Rick had kept. "Perhaps it was nothing more than an unhealthy kind of romantic interest. Still creepy and still wrong—but with no intent to murder. Still, I think you will agree he is now our strongest suspect for the murder of our beloved Hannah."

"How did he explain the notes?"

"After sputtering around, he claimed some utter nonsense about some *novel* he was writing. What a bunch of hooey." The police chief rolled his eyes. "He was writing *a romance,* he said, and he was taking notes on Hannah since a woman much like her would be central to his plot. Way too stupid to be true. I plan to question him again first thing in the morning, and I'd like you to be present."

Scott's fist was in a tight ball. "I would love to be there, sir."

As would I, I thought. But would it be too much?

"I have a lot of questions for the guy myself," Scott fumed.

"Be here at eight?"

Scott nodded.

"Hey, how are you holding up?" Matt's eyes went soft as he studied Scott. "This must be excruciating."

Scott reached over to touch my hand very lightly. "She was everything. It's hard."

"Well, I like to think she's watching over you, that they're still around somehow," said Matt. "That thought gave me some comfort when my mother passed. But she was in her eighties; she got to have a life." He sighed. "And for a girl like our sweet Hannah, life had just begun."

"Oh, I get what you're saying," Scott told him quietly. "And it's true that there are times I can feel her right here with me." He gave my hand a squeeze.

"Well, anything you need from me, you just say the word. And seriously, Scott, really awesome job on discovering that mail. And you were spot-on with your theory about Hannah and the stalker. You have a future here that's bright."

"I appreciate it." Scott looked down at the floor, embarrassed. He had, after all, had a little help.

"Okay, I won't keep you," Matt said. "I'll handle all the stuff underneath Rick's desk and get it back where it belongs. And we'll check it for his fingerprints lest he claim it was 'planted.' I'll let you concentrate on the investigation into Hannah's killer." He stood up from his desk and put an arm around Scott's shoulder. "See you in the morning, son."

As we walked down the hall, we held back on our comments, lest Scott appear to be a crazy man who was talking to himself.

"Sorry about that," Scott said in a whisper as he shut

his office door. "Taking credit for your work—but what could I do?"

"Matt wasn't wrong, you know. You *are* a great detective—and kind of sexy too."

When I leaned in for a kiss, he pulled me closer, and the kiss grew deeper before he broke away. "Hey, you can't go distracting the lead detective on your case." He kissed me again, but this time it was quick and gentle. "I do want more of this, but first I have a case to solve."

"I understand." I trailed my fingers down his chest. "What is our next step?" This felt good, like we were a team.

He sat down at his desk and pulled me onto his lap. "What I'm wondering," he said, "is whether Rick could have been the major player in this mail thing all along. Operating on that theory, was there anything you saw that might have made him worry that you had him figured out? That could have been a reason he'd want to make sure that you..." Scott looked down at his feet. "Well, that you could never talk."

I thought about it for a while then just shook my head.

"Maybe something small. Like if you saw him at a mailbox acting kind of odd. Or maybe at a bank. One of the tellers might have had some questions if he came in with a check made out to someone else. If you saw him giving an employee a hard time at the bank, just as an example, that might have worried him. Especially because you might mention it to me—since all of us on the force had knowledge of the case." He paused. "He would bring in the checks one by one—or a few at a time—not to arouse suspicion. Or he might have accounts at a variety of banks."

I thought about it more, but I still came up blank. "Nothing. I have nothing. I always tried to just ignore him if I saw him around town."

Scott's theory did, however, jog a memory of the last time I was in the bank, the time I ran into Toby. He had smiled and made some small talk—but just the minimum amount required to be friendly and polite. When he moved up in the line, I had been surprised at the huge stack of cash the teller counted out into his hand. That was the same week he had avoided me coming out of the flea market—where I knew not all the goods that people sold had been legally obtained.

Of course, it was not illegal for him to be in the flea market parking lot. Or to have large stacks of bills, which was the only form of payment some of the vendors at the market would accept. Plus, that was Toby's way: to be "chatty" while on duty and quieter—contemplative—when he was off the clock. It was like he had two selves, both of which I admired.

"Okay, this might be nothing." I described for Scott what was on my mind.

"Interesting," he said, "given the fact that this guy deals all day with the mail. It's not enough, of course, to bring him in for questions, but I'll keep that in mind for sure."

"I could check him out, pay a visit to his house perhaps?" Ghosts weren't bound by silly rules—"probable cause" and all of that.

"Well, it can't hurt," said Scott.

"Then that is what I'll do," I said, feeling guilty and apprehensive too. Could one of my favorite people in the world have been *stealing people's mail?*

Scott took note of my expression. "Hey, listen to me now." He put a hand on my cheek. "Nothing that you've told me means that Toby is a crook. We're just casting a wide net, keeping our minds open."

Then another recent memory hit me: Toby visiting the boxes on the street when it was well after dark. I had chalked it up to him needing daylight hours to go golfing and hang out with his buddies. This was, after all, a job for his "retirement" years.

And that could still be true! Toby did things his own way, but just to make myself feel better, I'd pop over to his house. Plus, I had been missing Toby. It would kind of be a way the two of us could "hang."

I stood up from Scott's lap and kissed the top of his head. "Stop by your place later on tonight?"

"We can order some Chinese," he said, "or do you want to catch a movie at the Yellow House?"

One more movie—at least—was on my bucket list, but it had been a long day.

"Let's play it by ear, okay?" I gave him a little wave as I slipped out the door.

CHAPTER TEN

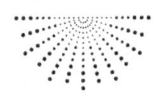

Toby's house was a white one-story brick with a neatly cut front yard. The bright blue front door was the only thing that set the house apart from the others on the street, the only special Toby touch. I helped myself to a vodka and cranberry juice. It had been that kind of day; it had been that kind of *week*. Toby, dressed in a gold bathrobe, was drinking one himself and already had the fixings out.

I looked around the room. Toby had a huge TV and was watching some documentary on the First World War while scrolling on his tablet. The room was very neat, with books stacked on all the tables, and the scent of garlicky tomato sauce wafted through the room. I made my way through the house to check out the other rooms—and it didn't take me long to find the thing I hoped I wouldn't.

In what appeared to be a spare room, opened boxes filled the twin bed and were spread out along the wall. I gasped as I moved in for a closer look. The boxes, partially wrapped in mailing tape and with stamps in the corners, contained the very things a thief would zero in on. There were phones and an iPad; there was an expensive-looking watch. Most heartbreakingly of all, there was a plastic container of sugar cookies with a little cursive note. *Love you lots! Aunt June.* The cookies had been lovingly decorated with swirls of colored icing and were surrounded by small baggies of other homemade treats.

I guess selling stolen items is more fun with a snack, I thought as a wave of disgust made my stomach drop. Knowing Toby and his quick mind, I figured he might have a system to unload most of the stuff even faster (and with less risk of exposure) than he could at the flea market. I moved back to the den to check out what he had up on his tablet.

Yes! He was selling things online. I watched, appalled, as he typed in a description of a high-end crystal vase.

I could see the headline now. "Mail Thefts Solved! Inside Job!"

Although the solving of it kind of broke my heart.

I moved through the house again. On the desk were stacks of envelopes filled with tax refunds, insurance checks, checks for graduations, checks for water bills. Two bottles of rubbing alcohol sat in the middle of the desk next to a wad of cotton balls. *Hmm.* I thought I knew his game. My eyes moved to a stack of checks on the left side of the desk; the names had all been rubbed off on the "Pay to the order" lines. Beside them was a stack on which Toby had replaced the names with his own.

My heart began to race as I thought about what I should do next. Legally, Scott would need to show that he had cause to go in and search the house. I picked up a few checks with Toby's name and stuffed them in my pocket. Perhaps they could be "dropped" by the wayward mailman and then be "found" by Scott, who could say he had a hunch he should keep an eye on Toby. The dates and dollar values could hopefully be used to match the "found" checks with the stolen ones.

For good measure, I headed to the den and peered once again at Toby's tablet. I texted myself the name of the site, on which Toby was typing in some details about a stolen phone while the television droned on about the Battle of the Somme. Luckily, I could see his user name, and I photographed the screen for Scott. I stood behind him patiently so I could get more pictures of some of his other listings. Then I went back into the room and photographed the boxes and the contents of the desk.

Scott—and Matt—would be glad to make an arrest on this one. The powers that be had left me here to solve my murder—and I had upped the game and solved a *bonus case* while I was on the job! (And it was apparently a case that had left the experts stumped.)

I headed out, and on a whim, I grabbed the box of treats, which still looked fairly fresh. I found a roll of tape on the desk and taped the box together as neatly as I could. Then on my way to Scott's, I made a little pit stop at 22 Blueberry Lane. I stuck the package in the box. *There you go, Aunt June.*

Some things I couldn't fix, but I'd fix what I could.

The next morning, Scott (and I) arrived a little early for the meeting with the chief and Rick.

Matt smiled wearily at Scott when we met him in the hall. "I'm still not sure what this means about Hannah's murder, but I have a feeling he'll fess up to masterminding the mail thefts. It will be a black mark on the reputation of our police department, but it will be one matter solved."

"Oh, yes, I can assure you that it won't be long before

we mark that case as solved," said Scott. "And you'll be glad to know the main guy wasn't Rick. I was just now in my office putting evidence together, and it all points to none other than one of our local carriers!" He produced the checks for Matt and told the story we'd come up with about how he had come upon them.

Matt studied them with interest.

"I have screenshots too of some of the stolen items he's put up for sale along with the user name under which he made the sales. I believe we have enough to do a search of the house and make an arrest real soon."

"Carlyle, you amaze me. We've just put you on the case, and now you've *solved the thing?*" He nodded toward his office. "We'll get to work on that just as soon as we are done in here with Rick."

Then we moved into Matt's office, where a dejected-looking Rick was already waiting, slumped down in a chair. Scott gently rubbed my shoulder, knowing how hard it must be for me to face my maybe killer.

"Morning, partner," Rick said, smiling at Scott weakly.

Scott's answer was a glare. Someone had brought in extra folding chairs, and Scott took a seat.

Then the chief strode in, and the three of them got down to business. Perhaps already knowing that his career was toast, Rick fessed up right away to taking packages and checks from the room where evidence was stored.

"It was wrong. I'm sorry. It's just that I can't seem to catch a single break these days." He nodded toward Scott. "This guy here gets the best assignments while I get relegated to the *jaywalking beat*? What kind of crap is that? So what if I took a box or two to give myself a little treat?"

Matt addressed him sternly. "I believe you know how big a deal it is for an officer sworn to uphold the law to 'treat' himself with stolen goods."

"What does it matter, really? No matter what I do, any case that's good would still go to Scott." Rick pulled off his badge and threw it on Matt's desk. "Here. I know you'll want this back." He let out a sigh. "Ever since the second grade, it always has been Scott. In spelling bees, the school play, it was Scott, Scott, Scott, Scott, Scott."

"So to even up the score, you took some of the mail that was in evidence," said Scott. "You wanted me to look bad. You wanted that stuff to go missing as soon as I came on the case."

"Well, a guy can try," said Rick. "It all came so easy for you. You even got the pretty girl who did those safety programs, the programs in the schools. So there's another thing to make you look good for the chief."

Scott leaped up and moved toward Rick. "Is that why you killed Hannah?"

Rick held up his hands. "I didn't kill that girl! No way! All I did was watch her, hoping she'd do something wrong so I could tell the chief. So I could make the 'perfect couple' look not so perfect after all."

Matt pulled Scott away, and Scott sat down beside me.

Then Rick sneered at Scott. "You know, you weren't the only one she was going out with," he said in a taunting voice. "You do know that, right?"

I gasped and grabbed Scott's arm. Of course, Scott would not believe him, but how dare he make that up about *someone's dead girlfriend?*

Scott managed to keep his cool. "I know nothing of the kind," he said.

"On the night she died, your girl was meeting up with some other guy. Guess she didn't think you were so hot after all." Rick looked really pleased to have delivered that big lie, but Scott was not about to rise to the bait.

"That simply isn't true." Scott reached out to squeeze my hand.

"Oh, yeah! I was watching. This guy came around a lot to her house after dark. Was always peering in her windows same as me—except he was more obvious about it. He must have liked your girl *a lot*."

"We are all aware of Bill Butterick and his interest in the victim. That isn't news to us," said Matt.

"Not the doughnut guy!" said Rick. "It was that guy who brings the mail."

"Toby Sykes?" Scott was on his feet. "Toby Sykes was watching Hannah?"

"I think they had something going." Rick's smile was pure evil. "I was watching Hannah on the night she died. I saw her leave the Yellow House and walk into the drugstore—and Toby Sykes was watching too, pulled up next to Hannah's car. Then she came out of the store, and that's when I saw this Toby get out of his car to meet her." Rick turned to glare at Scott. "I guess those two had *a date*. What do you think of that?"

"Did you see what happened next?" Matt was on his feet.

"Ah, no. I'd seen enough, so I just went on home."

Toby. I was shocked. And Rick could have saved me; he could have stopped my murder if he had not sped home like a fool right before it happened. Story of his life: never in the right place to "protect and serve."

But this time he almost had been.

Things moved quickly after that, and one of my

former favorite people in the world confessed to both my murder and the thefts. Apparently, he had the idea that I was onto him since I had seemingly appeared in all of the "wrong" places, as he explained to Matt. I'd shown up at the bank when he was there with a stack of stolen checks; I'd waltzed into the flea market during his trip there to unload some stolen stuff. Then I was at the diner when he was meeting with the young blonde to exchange a ring for cash. Surely I had heard the foolish woman going on and on about the two-carat diamond ring.

Given all of that, he couldn't take a chance on me putting everything together and going to my boyfriend, who was, after all, a cop.

Matt met privately with Scott right after his interview with Toby—and I, of course, was listening in.

The "friendly" mailman, it turned out, was full of many secrets. Rather than being a former executive on Wall Street, as he had always claimed, Toby was, in fact, on the run from an exclusive ski resort where he'd worked as a chef. After serving the rich and famous with their fancy clothes and cars, he'd gotten just the smallest taste of what the good life could be. And so he'd come up with a way to grab some of that for himself.

Specifically, he grabbed it right out of the business safe at the ski resort. He had carefully watched the movements of the manager, learning what his schedule was. Then he had made sure he was in the right place at the right time—and just out of sight—when the safe was opened and the manager dashed off to grab his buzzing phone.

When Matt left the room, Scott wrapped his arms around me. "Hannah, I'm so sorry," was all that he could say.

And that was the day I felt I died a little for the second time.

CHAPTER ELEVEN

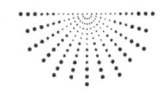

The next morning, I got up to make the coffee and found Celeste in my kitchen waiting quietly.

"You were right," I told her as a purring Nacho wound around my legs. "Maybe some of this is...better not to know."

She shrugged. "And you thought I was just being mean. Some of the rules, Hannah, are for your own protection."

I sat across from her, still somewhat in shock. "So up there, things are different? People don't pretend they're one thing, and then they turn around and do something...just *unspeakable?* I get to leave all of that behind?"

She smiled. "Where you are going, Hannah, there is

pure and utter peace. There is no earthly word to describe the way it feels."

"But there won't be Scott." A tightness filled my chest as I thought about his crooked smile, the little dimple in his chin. I had solved the murder, and I knew what that meant for me and him. "Have you come to take me *there?*"

Nacho meowed, insistent, and I got out her food and poured it into her bowl. "Here's the thing, Celeste. Mostly Scott and I were dealing with the murder, and there was no time for *us.* I am *so, so* thankful for the extra time, but could I have a *little* more, just to say goodbye to...goodbye to all of this?" To watch the stars with Scott and talk, to lay my head on his shoulder as we giggle at some movie, to breathe in the aroma of that first cup of coffee in the morning, to pop into Andi's house and press my face into Cleopatra's fur.

I looked into my Guide's eyes, almost reduced to begging. "Since the entry point at the Yellow House protects the living from *harmful* interference, could it really hurt for me to have a day—a week?" If it were not for Toby, I'd have fifty *years*.

But Celeste looked pained, and that did not bode well.

"Hannah, I'm so sorry," she said to me softly. "Spirits

are allowed to stay for specific purposes, and your purpose is fulfilled."

I collapsed into a chair. I had not told Scott goodbye.

"Of course," she continued, watching my expression, "it *could* be no one would notice if I gave you one more day. They're all so busy up there." She paused to think then gave me a wink. "Let's say I'll be back at ten a.m. tomorrow. Meet you back here then!"

With that, she disappeared. Which could be her way of saying, *"Don't try to argue with me."* Or perhaps it meant, *"Get on with your day, girl; start doing all the things."* Which I really should.

I changed into the yellow cotton dress that Scott liked the best, and within fifteen minutes, I was in his office. "You need to take the day off," I told him solemnly. "Today is…" I almost couldn't say it. "It's the last day that I get."

He shut his eyes and held them closed as if he could somehow wish away the words. Then he stood up from his desk and opened his arms to me.

Despite my bucket list, I found all I wanted was to be with Scott. We snuck Cleopatra out for a long walk in the park while Andi was at work. We sat on my porch and talked while Cleopatra dozed happily in the sun. We walked around the town, looking in the windows at all the stores I'd loved. We walked a lot that day. Scott and Cleopatra had been the best of buddies for a while, but she stayed close to me, and I liked to think she sensed that I was there.

Scott told me the whole town was shocked over the turn my case had taken. "No one can believe it."

"Well, at least they have their mail."

He put his arm around me as we walked slowly through the park. "Would it make you feel any better to know that Toby has been sobbing in his cell? That guy is the sorriest excuse there ever was for a human being, but at least he *understands* that he's a monster, Hannah. He knows what he did. Some of them are never sorry, just sorry they got caught."

When I myself began to sob, Scott stopped to hold me tightly. "Toby said the greed just overtook him, that he couldn't stand to think that he took your life." Scott pressed his face into my hair. "I can't stand it either," he said softly. "I can't believe you have to go."

A pure hate for Toby bubbled up in me, but there was no time for that. The changing light in the sky was a warning of how fast the day was passing. I pressed my lips to Scott's. "Let's not waste our time thinking about monsters. Let's think about us instead." I leaned in for another kiss.

For a while, we dropped the subject of the case while we enjoyed the day and tossed some sticks to Cleopatra, who ran after them with glee.

And then Scott remembered that he had an update for me. "This might make you feel a little better about the human race," he said. "As it turns out, Bill was telling me the truth about the reason he was at your house when he dropped the watch. He knew you had a stalker, and he was tailing Rick—much to Rick's chagrin." The information had come out as Rick was questioned further. More than once, Bill had threatened Rick and told him to back off. When Rick continued to hang out on my property at all hours of the night, Bill would be there too, making sure the rogue cop did not come after me.

"He didn't think we would believe him since Rick was one of us," said Scott. "Then after you were killed, I think he was afraid we would find his watch—and that it would point to him as the likely killer. Since it was engraved and all. Which is why he was so determined he had to get it back."

Hmm. Not all secrets were *bad secrets* after all.

"It was pretty brave of him to stand up to a cop like that." Scott gently squeezed my hand.

"Yeah. We still have no idea who this 'Saudade' might be, but now I'm pretty sure that Bill is not a killer, so I don't worry for her."

After some time in the park, we made our way to dinner at my favorite diner, where I could not decide between the spaghetti and the pancakes.

"If ever there was an excuse to get them both," said Scott with a smile, "I think you might have found it."

So I ordered my two favorites—or Scott ordered them for me. As far as the waitress and fellow diners were concerned, Scott was a man eating solo. He got more than a few sympathetic looks from those who knew his story.

If the gray-haired waitress was surprised when he ordered three entrees, she did not let on. "I will be back shortly with your dinner, sir," she said, tucking her pencil back behind her ear.

We devised a system where Scott appeared to be taking notes, "working" as he ate. From my place beside him, I could read his comments and his answers to my questions. Of course, I could chatter on, and no one could hear but Scott.

Just as we got our food and were digging in, Bill

came into the diner with Viola Tripp beside him. They were shown to the table just across from us, and the waitress dropped some menus.

"I wish that I could thank him," I told Scott as I watched Bill pull a chair out for Viola.

"This is so kind of you," she said. "I haven't ordered dinner from a menu in twenty years at least."

Then Scott did what I couldn't. He stood and held his hand out to Bill. "I want to thank you, Bill, for what you tried to do for Hannah."

Bill just shook his head. "What a treasure Hannah was, and how I surely wish I could have kept her safe."

"It was *my job* to protect her, to protect *this town*, and you did more than I could."

"I am sorry for your loss," said Viola solemnly. "I think that you and Hannah could have had a lovely future."

"Saudade!" said Bill.

"Saudade," Viola whispered.

"Saudade?" asked Scott. "Who is Saudade?"

"It's from the Portuguese," said Bill. "A melancholy longing for the things that one can never have." He smiled ruefully at Scott. "Story of my life."

Scott nodded to him sadly. "Thank you again. So much." He slipped back into our booth.

"I still don't understand," I said. "Was he longing for a mitten and a rubber duck?"

Scott shrugged, and we began to make our plans for the evening.

"One more movie," I told him. "I think that's what I'd like." One more time, I wanted to allow someone else's story to wash over me as I snuggled close to Scott.

Then my attention was diverted to the conversation next to us.

Scott caught my eye, and both of us stopped to listen.

"I would have never been a *boring* weatherman," Bill was saying to Viola. "I'd wear tiger ears to signal 'perfect weather for the zoo!' A rubber duck, you see, would have been my way to liven up bad news—that it was gonna be a wet one."

"They would have loved you, Bill." Viola dipped her spoon into her soup. "A man with the science know-how and a personality as well. You don't see that these days."

He sighed. "Then I would have come home to eat dinner and play a game of chess with my brilliant son. Or perhaps a brilliant daughter." He reached for a fry. "Did I ever tell you that I used to carve? I once carved a chess set." He dipped the fry in ketchup. "With a Star Wars theme! But one cannot play alone."

Scott gave me a knowing look as sadness filled his eyes. "Mystery solved," he wrote.

"I used to play that game." Viola took a spoonful of soup. "If you still have a set, I think I still remember most of the rules at least."

"Oh, yeah?" asked Bill, intrigued

After finishing our food, we headed to the Yellow House for my final film, a romantic, melancholy story that perfectly matched my mood. It was late when we came out, with only a few people milling in the lobby, as was typical after the last show on a weeknight.

I breathed in the popcorn smell for a final time and looked down for a last look at the blue stars on the carpet, which had become so familiar. Then I saw Arnie from the snack bar and an assistant manager rush in through the side door from the parking lot.

"I'll call the cops," said Arnie breathlessly before he registered that Scott was standing right there in the lobby. "Hey, Scott!" His voice was trembling as he made his way toward us. "There's a body out there in the very back where the employees park. I'm pretty *sure* she's dead. Because of all the blood." Arnie put a hand to his stomach as if he might throw up.

"Let's go. Show me now," said Scott as we followed Arnie out. Then Arnie pointed to a pickup truck and a pair of bloody legs sticking out behind it. The legs were very still.

"Go back inside and wait," Scott said to him calmly. "I'd like you to lock the doors. Don't let anybody leave. I will call for backup, and one of us will be in soon to question everyone."

I followed as he made his way to the truck, pulling out his phone and giving Matt the information quickly. "No sign of the perp," he said. "No witnesses that I can see in the parking lot."

"But wait." I grabbed his arm as he hung up. "The woman by the wall! She might have seen it happen." Then the woman turned, and I held on to Scott and gasped. "Oh, Scott, they hurt her too." Blood dripped from the woman's body, and her eyes were filled with shock.

Scott looked where I was looking. "Hannah, no one's there."

"Right there! In the blue blouse! Over by the wall!" *How could he not see her?* Then it dawned on me.

I ran to the trembling woman and put my arm around her. "It all will be okay," I said, trying to sound calm. "You're going to a special place, and I will be there too. I'll look for you there, okay?"

She looked at me, confused.

"Did you see who hurt you?" I asked her quietly.

"I was walking to the car. Just now. I was walking with my son! Then out of nowhere, I felt such a pain, like I've never felt before."

"Did you remember seeing someone right before it happened?"

She looked around her, dazed. "Well, yes, there was a young man. He had the blondest hair and one of those red shirts that say 'Pelham's Pizza.' I like to go there on the weekends sometimes with my son. But I can't imagine it was him who hurt me. He looked like a nice young man." Then she grabbed my hand and looked at me pleadingly. "Has someone called an ambulance? Because I think I'm really hurt. And have you seen my son? Is my son okay?" She looked down at the blood on her legs and her midsection. "I think I may need help."

"I will be right back," I called as I ran to Scott. "She was with her son!" I said, wondering why on earth the son would up and disappear. "And we have a suspect who was in the parking lot just before it happened. A young man with blond hair. A red Pelham's Pizza shirt."

Scott looked at me, wide-eyed.

I gazed down at the body. "I got all of that from her. Because she is like me. I can talk to her!"

"Are you the police?" The woman had trailed behind me, and she looked at me, confused. "You don't look like police."

Then I heard sirens wailing, and shortly after that, Matt was on the scene with two officers in tow.

I turned to find Celeste perched on the bumper of the truck.

I sat down wearily beside her. "So another one's come through."

"She won't be here for long. Mostly they just linger for a day at most, even at the Yellow House. You were the exception." Celeste studied the scene as Scott and a young officer put yellow tape around the scene and Matt photographed the body. "We believe the brand new spirit was allowed to stay to tell *you* her story." Celeste cocked her head to watch me. "It seems the universe has another mission for you—a mission here on earth." She looked down at her nails. "Which they say is super rare—for that to happen twice." She smiled to herself. "Look at me, a newbie Guide who gets assigned an extraordinary case—which makes me special too." She thought about it for a moment. "This was never hinted at in *How to Guide New Spirits to the Light with Love: A Primer for Beginners*. But whatever. It's all cool."

"So that means I get to stay?"

"Until this one's solved." She smiled.

This means I get to stay.

Scott put his hand on my shoulder. "Hannah, I'm afraid this will keep me pretty busy. Awful timing, really.

So this might be..." He was too choked up to finish. "What time do you have to go? We'll be at this pretty late, but maybe I can—"

"Scott! I need you over here," called Matt.

Scott blinked away the tears. "On my way!" he said.

I touched his arm. "I'll see you tomorrow. And probably the next day too."

"What are you saying, Hannah?"

"And I'll be here through the night—to help you catch this latest monster. You go do your thing, and I will see what else I can find out from the victim."

"So this is not goodbye?"

"Coming, Scott?" called Matt.

He looked at me, unsure.

"Go!" I said to him. "I'll see you soon—I promise. And I'll explain it then."

Thank you, universe, I thought, but I couldn't celebrate too much. Someone else had died too soon.

Still, the Yellow House was a special place. Its dead got to stick around to live out some final wishes and to see evil punished. Its dead got second chances—and I seemed to have a third.

I went back to the woman and put my arms around her.

"Am I dead?" she asked me in a halting voice. "I have a feeling that I'm dead."

"Did I tell you about the leaves?" I asked. "Silver, pink, and purple. So soft to the touch. They tell me we will love it."

And someday soon we would; I knew Celeste was right.

Soon, we would love it there in that other world—but for just a little longer, I would love it *here*.

# # #

Thank you for reading! Want to help out?

Reviews are crucial for independent authors like me, so if you enjoyed my book, **please consider leaving a review today**.

Thank you!

Penny Brooke

ABOUT THE AUTHOR

Penny Brooke has been reading mysteries for as long as she can remember. When not penning her own stories, she enjoys spending time outdoors with her husband, crocheting, and cozying up with her pups and a good novel. To find out more about her books, visit www.pennybrooke.com

Made in the USA
Coppell, TX
16 February 2023